THE BROKEN MIND SERIES

The Broken Mind Series

The Day the World Faded

BREN LEHOTAY

Brennan Lehotay

CONTENTS

ABOUT THE AUTHOR
vii

~ 1 ~

The Start of the Suffering
1

~ 2 ~

The Beginning of the Spiral
10

~ 3 ~

A Date Made
17

~ 4 ~

The Descent
27

~ 5 ~

The Emergency
48

~ 6 ~

The Revolver

63

~ 7 ~

The Recovery

65

~ 8 ~

A Fresh Start

70

~ 9 ~

A Means to an End

76

references

80

ABOUT THE AUTHOR

Bren grew up in Byesville, Ohio, and has always been passionate about mental health struggles, particularly in young adults. Bren got the idea to write this story when working with the youth of central Ohio and their struggles with adapting to behavioral health. While becoming a nurse Bren has achieved a Master's Degree in Nursing Leadership and Management, also has become a board-certified psychiatric mental-health registered nurse. This story is not one that is too dissimilar from many of the youth in todays world. Many youth do not have an outlet to understand that there is hope and help out in the world. With the skills that Bren has developed over nearly a decade in the field, they have been translated into a story to hopefully help someone in need.

Trigger warnings:

- Anxiety
- Anger issues
- Blood/gore
- Bullying
- Depression
- Eating disorders
- Anorexia
- Homophobia
- Paranoia
- Sexual situations
- Self-harm
- Suicide
- Trauma
- Schizophrenia

~ 1 ~

THE START OF THE SUFFERING

"Anything that's human is mentionable, and anything that is mentionable can be more manageable. When we can talk about our feelings, they become less overwhelming, less upsetting, and less scary." — Fred Rogers

"Hey." A strange voice echoed through the classroom. Marcus heard the voice and slowly looked over his shoulder and to his surprise, his friend Tyler was hunched over his desk, scribbling down everything that Mr. Leopard was saying, word for word. Clearly, Tyler hadn't whispered, given how lost in writing his notes he was, but Marcus couldn't help but feel a bit on edge by the words he heard either.

Tyler was a small, shy guy that was in most of Marcus' classes. He rarely spoke, as if he was slowly thinking everything that everyone said slowly and digesting everything. He had straight, blonde hair that hung around his face in such a way that it almost made him look more child-like. He was small for his age as well, although a fellow junior, he was only five-feet tall, which made even some of the girls outmatch him.

He watched him for a moment before turning his attention back to the teacher as well, presuming that he must have imagined it. Mr. Leopard, their teacher continued to drone on as Marcus watched with him with feigned interest.

Marcus was a popular sixteen-year-old junior in high school, top of his class. Everyone envied Marcus and he knew it. He had jet black hair that hung in tight, curls; framing his face perfectly and his eyes were a dark-catlike green. A rare feature that few people had; as most in the school were cursed with either blue or brown eyes. The striking looks that Marcus had, meant that he was a hit with the girls as well. Almost every day, one of them would compliment him on his eyes or ask to touch his hair (which he often declined). The attention was nice, although he only had eyes for one person. Marianne turned and smiled at him at that moment and he wondered if that was the small whisper that he heard; unable to identify the voice. He smiled back at her, before she swished her dark, brown ponytail and her blue eyes were placed back on the soul-sucking teacher that was Mr. Leopard. Marcus ran his eyes over the back of her, watching the way her waist shimmed as she crossed her legs and how her back went straight as she paid attention and started taking notes.

He had heard that she had a crush on him too, but he was still picking the right moment to ask her out (and there were not many moments when you were a student like Marcus). A part of him was certain that the right moment would come along at some point. Although, what that moment was exactly, he couldn't say, he just hoped that it would come by and right then and there she'd feel so enticed by him she'd have to say yes.

Marcus found himself trying hard to focus on Mr. Leopard. He had never particularly enjoyed English as a subject; although his father was an author. He thought English was rather dull and repetitive, yet his teacher continued to drone on and on about some old play that had been written over a hundred years ago. The teacher also seemed to favor Marcus as well, given his father's publications – although Marcus had the writing talents of a spoon.

It didn't help of course, for any of the students, that the English classroom was also the most unappealing classroom in the school.

In fact, Marcus was almost certain that rot was growing in the corners of it and Mr. Leopard was always ill, his droning voice often being matched with a slight wheeze or a cough. Not to mention there was almost no decoration other than the plain, cream walls of the classroom itself; almost as if the teacher wanted everyone in the class to know that they were in hell and would become bored to death.

Mr. Leopard was also not a very appealing man. His voice sounded like an owl in the way that it seemed to drawl on and on, like one hooting in the early hours of the morning – only interrupted by an occasional long sneeze, cough or a wheezing noise. In some ways, the teacher also looked like an owl as well; despite his name. In fact, Marcus found it funny in a way – the old, greying man didn't look like a powerful leopard that would stalk prey at all, more like an owl that would bore everyone to death with it's hoots.

Mr. Leopard's face was curved inwards slightly and his nose stuck out, long and sharp almost as if it was a beak. His eyes were also quite beady, like a birds as well and his hair all stuck out and up oddly; as if he had fluffed it. The glasses that hung on his long, beak-like nose didn't help the impression either, as it made them look wider and almost comical in a way. The teacher was also the only one in the school that dressed in a suit. It was a two-piece suit that seemed to hang off him, as if he never had the chance to get it fitted and looked like it was made of felt, rather than any actual materials.

"And that is why the King went mad. Now any questions? Do you think it's easy for anyone to descend into a state of madness? How do you think madness can be described in today's society? What do you think is the equivalent of madness? Do you think that perhaps mental health is a better word for it? How do-"

Just before Mr. Leopard was about to pick on anyone in the classroom, the buzzer went alerting everyone that finally, the most painful lesson of the day was over (Marcus was particularly thankful as he was almost certain that Mr. Leopard's eyes were narrowing expectantly on him and Marcus hadn't read any of the book that the teacher was harping on about).

The teacher sighed dramatically when the buzzer rang, as if he had just been about to give an awe-inspiring speech and this was the cruelest thing that had ever happened in the world. The sigh then turned into a cough and all the students hastily gathered there things, eager to escape the classroom.

As everyone packed up to leave, the teacher shouted after them. "Make sure that you all write down about how you think madness could be defined today! I want it by tomorrow's next lesson." He called.

Yet, with how fast everyone left the room, Marcus was certain that the teacher wouldn't expect anyone to actually bring in the home-work tomorrow; as they were all pretty much in the hallway and scurrying to their next lesson by then. He gleefully stuffed the book away into his backpack, knowing that he was safe for another day.

The hallway was far brighter and more well-kept than the English teacher's classroom. It was clear that when the school was origi-nally made, they had tried hard to make it seem like less of a prison for teenagers and had attempted to get them excited and involved in education. *A poor attempt really...* Marcus thought to himself, running his eyes over the hallway slogans.

The hallway was strung with sayings across the walls from famous artists, celebrities, historians or other notable figures in history. All of it was decorated with bright, curving letters; almost obnox-ious in the way it stood out in the hallway.

Life isn't complicated, or complex. It just is what it is and you get on with it. He thought, looking at some of the sayings about working past obstacles or hardship. Personally, Marcus had quite a nice life. His parents were quite well off, he had a good group of friends and he was planning to ask out his crush soon.

Things are good. He thought to himself.

Marcus strode straight to his metal locker, slamming his English books in there and thankful he wouldn't have to put up with the words of some long-dead playwright until tomorrow and quickly began taking out his math books instead. A lot of people found math hard, yet for Marcus they made sense and weren't full of "what ifs" and "yes, but" which was way better than any other subject.

Numbers were easy; numbers just had one meaning and one answer. It was rarely wrong. However, English – especially books – had many different meanings, different layers and many books rarely had one outcome or ending for the reader to interpret. Which made no sense to Marcus. Things should just be taken at face value; and that was that.

A lot like life. Things are good, things are simple. There is always a really straightforward and simple explanation for everything. Life isn't hard; it's like math. Marcus thought to himself.

Things should be as they are, it didn't make sense to have hidden layers to everything. In fact, he was relatively certain that the long-dead man who had wrote those plays would probably be laughing at his English teacher right now – trying hard to apply whatever his original meaning was to this and that. Things just are and that is that.

"Hey." Marcus shot around, his books in his hand, but as the students blended into their next class, he couldn't see anyone that was close enough for him to hear the faint whisper.

It was the second time he had heard someone whisper to him today, but he didn't think much of it. After all, he was popular and some of the girls couldn't always muster up the courage to talk to him; one of the many perks of enjoying attention.

Shrugging it off, he turned his attention to slamming the locker shut and making his way to the next class, dipping in and out of the students as he moved along the brightly colored hallways.

Albert Rosebird High was one of the lesser known schools in Columbus, Ohio. It was skirted on edges of the big city, but it was clear from the how modern and slick most of it was that they had tried hard to entice more parents shipping their kids off to the school. They wanted it to be more noticeable, to have more kids attend and to have more cheques their way (at least, that's what Marcus presumed). Yet, as it was further out of the center of the city, it ended up just having a smaller hive of students attending it instead.

Columbus itself was quite a large, thriving city. It almost hummed with the throb of people as they went about their daily lives. With a growing, large populous it also meant that it was quite loud and easy to get lost in the masses if you ventured into the city itself.

Yet, at high school, given it was just on the outskirts, everyone knew everything and your reputation was what made you who you were; and where you belonged int the status quo of things.

Marcus was lucky in a way; his parents were renown in the area and that made him popular. Everyone knew his family was rich, and his family name was spoken about in a hushed manner. Not to mention, he had very striking looks – which made the girls trip over themselves to talk to him.

Standing outside of the math's classroom, Marcus looked around, waiting for the teacher Miss Callie to arrive. Suddenly, Alexi stood in front of him, attempting to get his attention. *Ugh not again.* Marcus thought to himself. She gently ruffled his hair and tried adjusting his collar, with her freshly manicured hands, batting her long, mascara-clumped eyelashes at him.

"Alexi. No. I've told you enough times. Your parents would probably hate another suspension." Marcus said flatly, drawing away from her clutches.

Yet, she seemed unruffled, letting her hand drop to the side and putting on a melodramatic pout. She was a senior at the high, but she didn't act much older then any of the juniors; in fact, Marcus often thought that she was rather childish in a lot of ways. At eighteen years old, she was always getting into trouble for pushing people a bit too far.

Yet, she seemed to relish in the attention – as if any kind of attention was better than none. She loved people fawning over her or hating her. The boys loved it. The girls hated it. She adored it either way.

Some of the guys didn't mind attention from her, she was tall, blonde and had a typical hour-glass figure which a lot of the other girls envied. Although, instead of relishing in the envy, Alexi usually tried it on with them too; desperate to get with anything that moved.

Today she wore a short, pleated skirt (that she was often getting into trouble for, as it only just covered below her waist). She wore her shirt unbuttoned as far down as possible as well, showing just the hint of the top of her lace bra, which Marcus attempted to avoid looking at.

"You know one day you'll find me just too irresistible Marcus... I see it in your eyes." She murmured, tracing her finger from his neck to his lips. She leaned forward and Marcus' nose scrunched up smelling the unappealing scent of some dollar-store perfume that she was caked in. Marcus again slapped her hand away as her hands continued to trace over him and she huffed, turning away and pouting again.

Miss Callie suddenly turned up and unlocked the classroom door, letting the class spill into the math's classroom. The math's classroom was a lot more nicely decorated and colored than any of the others – at least in Marcus' opinion. The room was large and all the desks formed a big U-shape so that she didn't have to dip in and out of the desks and could clearly see everyone's work. On the walls were quotes of famous mathematicians and some math's jokes.

Marcus took his place in the center and started unpacking his books as Jerimiah took his place next to him. The chair squeaking as he sat down and started emptying his books on the table in a panic.

"Did you do the homework last night? I didn't..." Jerimiah whispered looking at Marcus his wide, brown, terrified eyes. Marcus snorted and nodded.

He knew Jerimiah well enough to know that he never did his homework. They had been friends for as long as Marcus could remember and Jerimiah was atrocious at math's; so bad in fact that he avoided doing it and then panicked whenever they had a lesson so he'd always be playing catch up.

For some people, like Marcus, math's made sense, and to others, like Jerimiah it didn't – but again, that was just the way it was, and Marcus didn't mind helping out his friend.

Marcus slid his homework that Miss Callie had assigned the day before onto the desk and whilst her back was turned Jerimiah started scribbling some of his answers onto his homework sheet; taking care to make some obvious mistakes as well, so he wouldn't get pulled for copying.

Jerimiah wasn't very academic, in fact the two boys were polar opposites in a lot of ways, but that didn't stop them from being close friends. Jerimiah was quite tall, like Marcus and he had brown, floppy hair that drooped over his brown eyes and tan skin. Although he wasn't particularly good with academic studies like math's or English, he did exceptionally well with anything that required his hands.

Due to that, usually with any of the extra classes they had to take for credits Jerimiah usually helped Marcus with. He often helped Marcus with woodworking, pottery and other things that involved a steady touch. Marcus was terrible at all of them, and his teachers often compared him to that of a child who couldn't even pick up a pen.

Miss Callie turned to address the class and slowly Jerimiah slid the paper back to Marcus. He grinned to himself as he looked over at his friend. They had been friends for as long as Marcus could remember and although they were very dissimilar, Marcus couldn't imagine a life without his friend.

"Right, can you all pass your homework to the person sitting next to you and we'll get to work. Open page 62 of your textbooks..."

She said, tucking a stray hair behind her ear.

The math's teacher was very pretty, she had silvery-blonde hair that she plaited and fell down to her waist. She didn't look the part of your stereotypical math's teacher either; she often wore dresses that were quite floaty or airy, that swam down to her ankles. Her eyes shone a bright blue and seemed to shine with intensity and passion whenever she explained equations, or walked the class through a new mathematical concept. She was Marcus' favorite teacher for that; although admittedly, he had a bit of a crush on her as well.

"Hey... Marcus..." Marcus looked around the class, again trying to see where the strange whisper that he just heard had come from. Yet, all eyes were either on the teacher or the textbook.

~ 2 ~

THE BEGINNING OF THE SPIRAL

"My dark days made me stronger. Or maybe I already was strong, and they made me prove it." — Emery Lord

Marcus tried to ignore the whispers, in fact he was almost certain that it was just one of his friends messing with him. Or that someone had tried talking to him and he couldn't distinguish who at the time. Or perhaps even, there was a girl that had a crush on him that had a mousy little voice and attempting to make conversation, but he couldn't see where it was coming from.

Yet, the whispers started persisting and he realized, in fact, it made sense that something strange might be going on. For now though, Marcus wasn't going to give it too much attention, as he had other things to worry about. In particular, his mind kept racing to Marianne, the way she'd shimmy in her chair, that smile she had given Marcus earlier today, and how exactly he would be able to ask her out...

He trudged to the usual hangout spot; the soccer field nearby the school. It was usually quite busy in the summer, but considering they were now entering autumn, people were less enthusiastic about going out in colder weather and it was almost empty for

Marcus and his other classmates to enjoy playing soccer until the sunset.

There was also another benefit of going outside when it was getting colder. In fact, Marcus preferred cold weather – especially the fall. In fall, when you walked you could hear the satisfying crunch of leaves beneath your feet and watch as the sun started dipping further down, the days becoming shorter.

He arrived at the usual spot and quickly took off his school shoes, putting on his trainers and stripping off his jumper.

The large soccer field was about a ten-minute walk from the school and was at quite a high point in the city of Columbus, it overlooked the entire city. The lights and the hum of the city moved around from below the large field and Marcus watched it as he rolled up the sleeves of his shirt.

He enjoyed the view for a moment, before turning his attention to the large, stretch of field itself to see if anyone else had beaten him to it and had started playing.

He could see Maury in the distance kicking a ball to Tyler and Jerimiah. They scurried about, laughing heartily with one another, trying to dodge one another's tackles or kicks. Yet, Marcus noticed that the other boys that had joined them today from school watched on with sour expressions a bit further away, so Marcus jogged over to help set things right and get everyone involved.

Maury was the only gay at the school. Marcus didn't care. Jerimiah didn't care. Tyler didn't care. However, everyone else at the school tried to ignore him as if it was infectious, or they were terrified he'd sprout a pair of wings and horns. Maury found it hilarious and often joked or flirted with the boys that seemed to be repelled by him. Offering them over for sleepovers.

He was out and loud about; which definitely seemed to unruffle a lot of people in the school – and sometimes it wasn't only the students that seemed to look at him distastefully. The boy was lanky and had short, blonde hair that seemed to stick out in tufts. He was always well-dressed and whilst he did seem a little more feminine compared to the other boys, he still played soccer just as well as anyone else and often joined in on the boys video game nights too with Marcus, Jerimiah and Tyler.

As soon as Marcus jogged over, the rest of the boys came to join the small group as Marcus started sorting everyone into teams. It always fell the same – Marcus was with Maury so there would be no foul play and Jerimiah on the opposite team to make sure that they didn't try and hurt either of them. It was exhausting sometimes, making sure everyone played fair; but he looked out for his friends and he was certain that if the roles were ever reversed they would do the same.

Quickly, the boys set about playing and Marcus was pleased that he had scored a few goals already. Yet, Marcus started noticing that the other boys were tripping Maury up which immediately made his anger flare.

Why can't everyone just act nice for one fricking day? It's not that hard and it's just a game after all. He thought bitterly to himself.

"Can you stop that? You're ruining the game for everyone." Marcus had told them flatly a couple of times, as the sunshine began to dip lower and lower, slowly turning afternoon into evening.

The city below the field had also begin to slow from rush hour to a steady flow. Streetlights and buildings flickered on, casting the city into a steady, golden and orange glow.

Marcus pulled them altogether for one last time and warned them that if anyone else was tripped up, he wouldn't be playing for at least a few good weeks. He'd had enough of them being childish with Maury and his friend deserved better treatment.

Then, suddenly, Marcus was tripped up by Jerimiah when he was about to score and his anger flared up, almost drowning him.

"What the hell man! What is wrong with you?" He yelled, pushing Jerimiah off him. The boy looked hurt for a moment, but quickly turned it into a grin.

"Don't you know the point of soccer?" Jerimiah said jokingly, pushing him back and laughing heartily.

Yet, Marcus couldn't see past the sudden anger that had flagged up inside of him. All he wanted was to play a game of soccer after school with his friends and not only were they acting weird with Maury, but now he had been shoved by his best friend – it was just too much; especially as he was grappling with how best to approach the Marianne situation.

He was dismayed with how his friend had acted and how he had clearly ignored what he just asked. He just wanted everyone to get along and as he had tackled Marcus, he was certain the rest of the team would use it as an excuse to pick on Maury.

"Get off, I'm done." He snapped back, shoving Jerimiah onto the ground.

Jerimiah simply looked up at him, hurt and confused as to why his friend's anger seemed to flare out of nowhere.

"Calm down man, you're acting weird." He said gently, getting to his feet and dusting himself off.

The other guys crowded round them both wondering if they were about to witness a fight, when Marcus just turned on his heel, stomping off and heading home. Not willing to talk about it further or engage with his friend. He needed to cool off and been surrounded by a group of boys that would no doubt egg them both on to fight.

"Hey... Marcus." He whipped around, to look at the crowd of boys, but sure enough they were all just staring at him confused from his outburst, yet seemingly respecting his decision to leave and not a single one of them uttered a word.

*

Marcus sat down at his desk in his room. He was quite lucky in a lot of ways, his parents lived in a large house and had quite high paying jobs in the city, which meant that Marcus was lucky enough to get pretty much whatever he wanted. He was always respectful of what he asked for though and worked for what he wanted if there was anything in particular he'd ask for.

The other kids knew that he was quite well-off and because of it a lot of them often sucked up to him, hoping that he'd get them things or buy stuff. Yet, after many years of being betrayed by people or having them act two-faced, he had been able to filter out the people who just liked him for the money that lined his pockets and nothing more.

Overall, Marcus was a pretty well-off teenager that could get whatever he wanted. Yet today, he didn't want anything, not even dinner and he'd asked if his parents could leave him alone to his studies, so they'd obliged. The days events kept replaying in his head and he tried to ignore it as Jerimiah's face kept flashing up with a sense of hurt flashed over it.

Jerimiah was his oldest and best friend, they rarely fell out and when they did, they made up shortly after. However, today Marcus didn't really want to make up with him. He felt hurt by his friends actions and disappointed in how he'd acted with him.

Marcus skimmed his room, bored and finding himself unable to focus. His room was quite large, it had a desk, a double bed, a TV, a computer and a games console. He'd even managed to convince his parents to let him keep a mini-fridge in there, which was currently whirring and stocked full of sodas. Marcus wheeled his chair over to the mini-fridge and snapped open a can of soda, carefully looking at his math's homework set from today and trying to readjust his focus.

But... there was something different about today. It was like the numbers were refusing to cooperate with him and he kept staring off into space and getting lost in thought; almost like his mind couldn't stay in one place. He usually really enjoyed math's, in fact it was one of the only things that he was really good at, yet the more he tried to concentrate the harder it seemed.

Slowly, irritability started to bubble up inside of him. *Why is it so difficult to concentrate? It's just numbers! I'm good at numbers! Why won't they make sense like usual?*

Eventually, frustration boiled over and he scrunched up the homework and chucked it to one side. Suddenly, his phone started pinging. He looked over it to find a load of texts from Jerimiah.

Hey man, u ok?

Sorry if I annoyed you today.

Text me back when you get chance, let's talk yeah?

Instead of responding, he went to switch his phone off and put it on charge, when someone else texted him and his heart skipped a beat.

Hey, I heard that you fell out with Jerimiah today. Are you okay? Here if you need to talk at all.

News really does travel fast at high school... Marcus thought. Yet, he couldn't help but feel happiness swish inside of him when he realized that Marianne cared enough to check up on him. He tried to contain his excitement and re-read the text a couple more times over before deciding how best to respond.

Marcus had known that he'd liked Marianne since he first met her. They were four years old and she was crying because someone had taken a cupcake she was going to eat for her dessert at lunch time. So, Marcus had given her his brownie that his mother had made him for his, and they had been friends ever since.

Yet, Marcus hadn't wanted to be friends, he had known even from that young age that he had a crush on her. He wanted to be around her as often as possible and sad when she wasn't there. He thought that she was absolutely beautiful; and longed to play with her hair and kiss her. Yet, even though he had known her for as long as he had, he'd never found the right words to ask her out or the right moment to do so.

Settling on the right words to type, he waited a couple of second as to remain 'cool' then texted her back.

I'm okay thanks, just a normal falling out on the soccer field. Happens every week or so. How're you?

He watched his phone eagerly, watching three dots pop up as she started typing back and smiled to himself. *She's clearly eager to talk to me as well if she's texting back this fast...* Marcus thought to himself.

Not bad. My mom keeps sending me dresses she thinks I should wear to the formal later this year. I think they all look trash. See any you like?

She then started sending pictures of dresses to him and his heart seemed to do a flip as he imagined interlinking her arm and attending the formal with Marianne wearing one of the dresses. They were all quite extravagant and looked almost like princess-dresses.

She is a lot like a princess in a lot of ways... Beautiful, kind and smart... He closed his eyes and pictured them together, before grinning and looking back at his phone again.

He texted back, saying that she'd look amazing in any of them, and then grinned to himself as he realized exactly what he was going to do and how to ask her out.

Marcus had waited years to have the perfect plan to ask her out and now he had one, at last. He was going to ask her to the formal in another month, nearer the date, and then he was going to ask her to be his girlfriend during the formal's first dance.

Yeah... That will work. Girls love romance and stuff... She'll definitely say yes if it's during a dance.

He looked at the time and realized that it was growing late. Switching his computer off, his television and phone, he got changed into some pajama bottoms before rolling into bed. Yet, he found that now, he was struggling to sleep. He stared up at the ceiling for awhile, wondering why he couldn't settle down.

Is it because I fell out with Jerimiah? Or because Marianne texted me? His thoughts blurred and meshed together, as he started tossing and turning in bed, unable to get uncomfortable. Eventually he started drifting off to sleep when he heard it and he knew that he was not going to be able to sleep at all.

"Hey... Marcus... We're watching."

~ 3 ~

A DATE MADE

"If you have been brutally broken but still have the courage to be gentle to other living beings, then you're a badass with a heart of an angel."
— *Keanu Reeves*

Marcus walked into the high school and looked like he might drop at any moment. He hadn't slept a wink of sleep all night and the bags under his eyes seemed to be almost grey, they were so dark and large that they made his green eyes seem almost like specks on his face.

He seemed to float through the day like a zombie, not really paying attention to anyone or anything; although he could hear a constant chatter of whispers around him with his name. He'd look around, but could find nobody close enough for him to hear them whispering and decided that he was probably going mad.

Mr. Leopard had again started telling them about a the king in the play that he was reading, and how he was going mad; that sane moments were only given here and there as he started making snap judgements and decisions that ultimately led to him spiraling.

As much as Marcus tried to focus though, the less he could. His tiredness was too overbearing and it was hard enough to stay awake during class. Luckily, the teacher seemed to sense that Marcus was a bit less focused then usual, and picked on everyone else other than him.

The rest of the day rushed past quickly; something which Marcus was thankful for – slow days tired were something that he wouldn't even wish upon his worst enemy.

It was just before his favorite class (although, admittedly he was dreading it as he hadn't done the homework and was going to be sat next to Jerimiah who he'd ignored since yesterday) when Maury was undoing his locker nearby. He nodded to him, not necessarily wishing to interact, as Marcus wanted nothing more than the day to be over and go to bed; feeling groggy and disorientated.

Then, all of a sudden George came out of nowhere and slammed Maury's face into his locker forcefully, giving Maury a bloody nose, as he slunk down the locker, holding it as blood started gushing out of his nose and trickling onto his white shirt. The bully grinned maliciously and rose up to kick the boy when Marcus stepped between them.

He was tired, he was done for the day, but he wasn't going to let someone hurt his friend.

George was a pain and mostly picked on Maury and Tyler in their little group. He was large, muscled and always wore a scowl on his deep-set face. His stony-blue eyes seemed to reflect years of resentment and rage that had built up over a distressing home situation, and his hands were calloused and seemed to have permanent bruising from hitting many a peer.

"You protecting your boyfriend now huh? Why else would you defend a boy bumping ass like this?" George said snidely, puffing his chest out like a cobra rising up, ready to snap and bite.

"He's my friend and you're going to leave him alone." Marcus said flatly.

He'd had barely any sleep, he was going to get told off for not doing homework by his favorite teacher and he'd fallen out with his best friend. The last thing he needed was this, but he couldn't just stand by as George unfairly landed hits or punches on his friend – after all, he may be feeling miserable himself, but he wasn't going to let anyone else feel the same.

"You know I could beat your ass in two minutes flat so why don't you step out the way whilst I take out the gay trash here. Guys should date girls and doing anything other than that is disgusting. He should be locked up." With that George spat on the ground, as if even saying the word *gay* was an insult to his mouth.

Yet, Marcus didn't move and shook his head. He knew for a fact that George wasn't going to hit him in front of everyone, Marcus was well liked, popular and above all – he played on the soccer team, which meant that in particular the coach had his back and would be very vindicative in gym class if he was suddenly unable to play. Yet, it seemed that George was willing to call this bluff, as he swung a punch at Marcus.

He ducked, just in time and suddenly an annoyed and curious Mr. Leopard appeared from his drab English classroom to look around the hallways. George leaned forward, grabbing Marcus by the scruff as his collar as he leaned into the locker, taking care to turn to the side to make it look like the boys were just having a simple conversation if the teacher was to look down the hallway.

"Meet me outside the school at five. You're going to wish you didn't do that." With that, the boy let go of Marcus and shoved him back, so he fell into the locker and almost tumbled over Maury. George disappeared into the crowd of the other students and Marcus sighed, stepping over Maury and opening his locker to shove his books inside.

Maury got up on his feet, dusting himself off and watching Marcus carefully. He almost looked embarrassed in a way, as if he felt ashamed that someone had even needed to step in and stick up for him.

"Thanks." He said quietly, turning to his locker again and grabbing some tissues out of it.

"Don't mention it. Please don't tell your sister. Alexi gives me enough attention as it is and it's already hard pieing her off." Marcus said, his voice thick with exhaustion.

Maury laughed heartily, readjusting his uniform and patted Marcus on the back.

"Your secret is safe with me." He said, dabbing his nose and trying to stop the bleeding as he walked to the next class.

*

Marcus looked at his phone, biting his lip as he waited outside the school. A part of him didn't want to do this at all, in fact if he wanted to he could just leave. Yet, he had said he'd meet George here and he was determined to teach the bully a lesson, to make sure he didn't pick on his friends again.

Why does he hate Maury so much? Yeah he's gay and he likes guys, but what's wrong with that? It's not like he's been all over George. In fact, he's very clearly never liked George. Marcus thought to himself, puzzling over it all.

Maury told me you stuck up for him today. You're a hero <3

Surprised to see such a thing, he had saved the text and began grinning to himself. He did have quite a crush on Marianne and seeing that she thought of him as a hero had given him more incentive to make sure that he would survive this fight and make George pay for what he did.

He was thankful that Maury hadn't told Alexi, after all he couldn't stand the way she touched him and seemed to be all over him sometimes. A lot of the other girls were direct in their crushes towards him, but Alexi was different. She was very handsy and very forward; in particular it was almost like she showed affection through touch. Which Marcus didn't judge her for, but he didn't like it personally and he didn't want to give her more incentive to try and sloppily be all over him.

Marcus' mind steadily turned back to George. He was a bully and hated across the school by everyone; even a couple of the teachers. He was someone that seemed to relish in dolling out punishments and physical injuries to anyone that so much as looked at him sideways or didn't agree with him. Like most bullies, there wasn't a set rulebook on things to say or do that could help you avoid such a beating from him – simply existing in a way he didn't like was enough to incur his wrath.

Tyler and Maury were often in the firing line of George and Marcus had intervened many a time before, yet usually he'd had Jerimiah at his side... unlike today. A part of him regretted falling out with his friend, but he was still a bit annoyed in the way he had tackled him the day before. He wasn't ready to forgive his friend yet, in fact a part of him was certain that if he never tackled him this would have never have happened.

Instead, Jerimiah and Marcus may have walked to class together and with Maury there as well, George would no doubt have disliked those odds and kept moving. He may have even chosen easier prey, far outside of Marcus' line of sight and he wouldn't be stuck in this mess.

Slowly Marcus turned it all around in his head, he was upset but he still needed to fight. Although, exhaustion had well and truly started settling in, much more powerful than before and he almost felt lucid in how drained he felt. Yet, Marcus presumed that it would make him invincible in a way, after all if he was too tired to think or feel things properly, he had no doubt that he could beat George easily.

It was strange being outside of the school long after everyone had gone home, there was a heavy quiet that hung in the air, where it was usually buzzing with noise and students. In fact, the quietness anywhere in Columbus was rare, the city was constantly full of noise, people and things.

The season seemed to add a chill to the air as well, and Marcus found himself drawing his jacket closer around his chest and shivering, before again looking around to see if the bully was anywhere close. He looked at the school as the day slowly turned to dusk and realized how strange it looked, with the sun dipping behind it and the sky slowly fading to a dark, navy blue.

He shuddered again and looked around. Marcus presumed that the ominous quiet was preparing him for a fight – much like a boss fight in a video game. Usually, when he was playing games, it would go oddly quiet whenever he was about to take down some-one big and it felt the same today.

Sure enough, George seemed to appear in front of him, almost like a ghost. Yet Marcus appeared unruffled; instead he stood taller, puffing his chest out and squared his feet. He was going to make this bully think twice about doing something like this again.

"You know you don't have to do this man, why do you even want to fight me? You know it was wrong to hit Maury earlier." Marcus said, pulling up his fists to block his face.

George laughed at him, as if Marcus had just tried to explain that the sky was green instead of blue. It was cold and malicious, almost biting in the way that the chuckles fell across his tongue.

"You're standing up for a guy who sucks off other guys. A guy that goes against basic *human nature.* That makes you just as sick and deluded as him." George said, spitting at him as he spoke.

As he wiped the spit off his face in disgust, Marcus noticed that the boy must have gone home to change. He wore a dark, red hoodie and some tattered jeans. Without prewarning, he threw a fist at Marcus who darted back.

"See? You can't even take a punch like a man." George retorted, snorting.

"That's because you throw like a little boy." Marcus quipped back.

George seemed to flush red with anger, and in that moment he began advancing on Marcus. He started raining punches anywhere he could get in edgeways whilst Marcus blocked them and fought back ferociously.

Both boys were obviously not talented in the art of fighting and punched, kicked, spat and hurled insults at one another as they fought. Within just under ten minutes, Marcus had a bruised eye which he was sure would turn black in a few days and George was clutching his side, where Marcus was certain he probably bruised a few ribs.

Suddenly, they lurched at each other and were biting, kicking and hitting whatever flesh either one of them could hold, when a whistle was blown and they were ripped off each other. Hands circling Marcus' waist forcefully.

"I'm disappointed in you." Miss Callie said.

Marcus was shocked to find that two police officers had apprehended them both and Miss Callie was looking down at both of the young boys, yet her eyes looked both hurt and betrayed as she stared at Marcus.

*

Marcus sat uncomfortably in the principal's office with the principal, two police officers, his parents, his coach and Miss Callie. Every now and then someone would throw a pitying glance at Marcus, but it didn't last long and was quickly replaced with a scowl.

The office itself clearly wasn't meant to accommodate this many people and in a way Marcus felt surrounded and hounded by the sheer number of adults around him. He'd passed George on his way into the principal's office, who was looking down at the floor with a scowl and avoiding everyone's gaze, with what Marcus guessed were his parents.

The office was decorated in a slick-black modern décor, as if the principal wanted to pretend he was not in the dark ages, and in fact, 'down with the kids' but everyone knew it was further from the truth. The principal even had an open-door policy, but everyone stayed far away from him as they all knew his views were old-fashioned and seemed to hinge on preaching sometimes.

"You know this school has a zero-tolerance policy to violence and bullying right?" The principal said, leaning forward and closely inspecting the young man sat behind his desk, flagged by his parents on either side.

The principals voice was deep, yet sharp. He was dressed in a fine, modern suit and was wearing a tie. Marcus had been pulled many a time into the office before, but never for a fight and he felt a rush of anxiety bubble inside of him whilst the principal awaited an answer.

In a lot of ways; Marcus was a prized student. His parents were quite well off and regularly made donations to the school, he was the star player on the soccer field and he was great at math's in particular. The principal seemed to find it hard to dismiss him, but there seemed to be something lurking beneath the surface; as if it was obvious the reason why he was in this mess in the first place.

Marcus tried to speak and opened his mouth, ready to explain that George was in the wrong. However, the anxiety seemed to overwhelm him for a moment and instead he found he couldn't say even a word, as if something had tied up his tongue. So, he nodded slowly, disappointed in himself and where all this sudden worry and panic had come from and stared at the principals black, plain desk.

"You are a star student both in class and in the soccer team. You could win many a scholarship and yet you've tried to throw it all away for what? The sake of one fight? It's a shame Marcus, a real shame.

It's not good enough at all and you know it. We have a zero-tolerance policy and you should have never attempted to fight this young man on school grounds or outside of them, no matter what he did. If you were being bullied, or if one of your friends were, you should have gone straight to a teacher instead." The principal said, in an almost patronizing tone; like he was chastising a child instead of a teenager.

Marcus looked up at him and the hate seemed to simmer from his eyes to the principal. Maury had been attending the school for same amount of time as anyone else, yet all the teachers turned a blind eye whenever he was attacked, spat on or bullied in any way.

In fact, when Maury had gone with a nosebleed to his next class – apparently nobody had batted an eyelid. Luckily, Marianne was also in his science class at the time and had helped him clear up his nose. *It's disgusting of these people… They preach that everyone is treated equally and apparently have this zero tolerance policy; but they only make it work for where they see fit – and it's never in the right places.* Marcus thought bitterly to himself.

He was pretty sure that the school didn't care; in fact he was sure that some of the teachers were homophobic as well as George and were deliberately turning a blind eye towards any violence or whenever one of the kids were trying to defend it, but it was his word against theirs and from experience it was rare that adults would listen to him… Or to any other teenager in the school for that matter.

"I heard Maury had tried to talk to you a few times." Marcus said, his teeth clenched and unable to hide his true feelings about the matter.

He's been in this office. He's spoken to Jerimiah and I about it multiple times. Are you really going to sit here like the terrible principal we all know that you are and pretend that I'm in the wrong? Why don't you do something about your school to make it a safer place for everyone? He thought, wishing he had the courage to say it out loud.

The principal watched Marcus, as if he could read his thoughts and knew exactly what he was saying. Instead of acknowledging what Marcus had just said, or even answering the clear question that hung in the air about it, he simply clicked his teeth together and shook his head.

"We've got a no-tolerance policy in the school. You and George are suspended with immediate effect for the next two weeks." He said defiantly.

The entire crowd looked on at the principal in shock and Marcus' parents and the coach went to protest. Yet the principal held up a hand in front of them all.

"Don't make me turn this into three weeks. Now leave my office." He said.

With that he gestured the small crowd to his door to leave and waved in George and his parents.

~ 4 ~

THE DESCENT

"Anyone can be affected, despite their level of success or their place on the food chain. In fact, there is a good chance you know someone who is struggling with it since nearly 20% of American adults face some form of mental illness in their lifetime. So why aren't we talking about it?"
— *Kristen Bell*

Marcus sat in front of his parents and tried hard to mask how he was feeling. He was still exhausted and even reeling from the days events and the last thing he wanted after such a long day was to be chastised by them too.

They were all sat inside of his father's study and he was sat in front of his fathers desk. In a way, he felt like he was being told off all over again – the way both of his parents stared at him with their eyes glowering.

His father was a well-known author in Columbus and had written many books – possibly a reason why Mr. Leopard seemed so encouraged to have Marcus in his class (although Marcus could barely string a sentence together). Behind the study where his father sat, was a bookshelf, strung with many of the books his father had written. They were all various different things – some thrillers, other murder mysteries, some crimes. He was known as a 'modern day Shakespeare' according to a lot of columnists in the city, but Marcus didn't see it. In fact, he found most books incredibly boring and struggled to focus on it.

His father looked down at Marcus with round, large glasses (which Marcus was almost certain his father didn't actually need and wore them for aesthetic purposes; yet instead it just made him look pretentious) and straightened his tie, a clear sign that he was about to go on a long rambling lecture.

His mother on the other hand seemed to straighten her back, as if she were about to point her fingers and nod along with his father. She wore a pencil dress, and was drawn up – looking disappointed. She was a beauty mogul in the city, responsible for various beauty products and skincare ones that made his parents quite the power couple; and it was clear that they did not approve of having to be drawn away from their work to deal with Marcus' seemingly petty problems.

He fidgeted in his seat, which creaked as he shifted. His father had the leather chair, but Marcus – given what punishment he was about to receive – was resigned to the mahogany chair that matched his father's desk. Marcus braced himself, ready for whatever punishment and yelling was about to be doled out.

Yet, they both surprised Marcus with what they said next.

"We're proud of you for sticking up for your friend. We know that the school often turn a blind eye to Maury when he was being bullied, and it's kind of you to stick up for him." Marcus raised his eyebrows in shock at his father's words. For the first time in front of his parents, he found himself speechless as he watched them in shock.

He certainly wasn't expecting to be praised for such a thing, especially given the schools zero tolerance policy, which he had so bluntly flaunted and defiled. In fact, he hadn't just defiled it – he'd jumped well over the line and he'd beaten someone up just as badly as they injured him and his friend.

"However, there are some things you should know about George and in future we don't want you to engage in any fights or talk to him. Please ignore him.

His family is very different to ours, he lives in a very bad neighborhood and his father is a well-known alcoholic. He hits his wife and George often; he's learnt from this environment which is how he takes out his feelings.

You're a good kid, with a bright future and because you're a good kid, you should understand never to bring this up with him. We're telling you this, as parents, so that you understand better why he acts the way h does.

He's a sad, young boy with very little prospects – it's hard growing up an environment like that and the only way out is using your fists. So stay away from him, keep your head down.

Now, for the next two weeks, since you're off school, we expect you to keep the house tidy, run some errands for us and take some online classes instead. We clear?" His father said, crossing his arms and leaning back in the leather chair, sat behind the long, mahogany desk.

Marcus was shocked by how nice his parents had acted about it all, yet he also felt sorry for George in a way.

He couldn't imagine having parents who hit him; even when Marcus was a child, his parents had always used their words to explain situations and had tried hard to teach Marcus to do the same, so that he never wanted to use his fists. Yet, it was clear that they understood why he had done so on this occasion.

He nodded, and reluctantly resigned himself to his room, switching on his television and collapsing into bed. Ready to fall into a blissfully long and dreamless sleep as the television provided a gentle hum of noise in the background.

"Marcus... Marcus... Your parents are angry with you... They're lying about how they feel."

Marcus shot up, and looked around the room, he couldn't see anyone. He took his phone out of his pocket, and although he had a lot of unread texts from people, nobody had tried calling him.

He was tired; delirious even... That must be it. He hadn't slept properly over the last two days and that was clearly taking a toll on him.

Yet, he couldn't argue with that voice, wherever it had come from – and now he was too awake and stressed to fall asleep. *Wherever that voice came from, it's right. My parents are angry with me – that I fought back. That I didn't use more of my words. After all; that's what dad always says... To try and use my words more...* Marcus thought, rubbing his eyes.

He settled back down on his bed, knowing now that he was gong to be unable to sleep. With that he flicked the channel on and instead tried to focus on the television set. The show that had flickered on was about a guy who had supernatural powers, and everyone around him was slowly being replaced with copies of themselves; and it was the guys job to try and stop them all.

The guy, named Colin, was trying to figure out if one of his friends had been replaced with a copy. When a glimmer of darkness came over their eyes. Sure enough, the main character whipped out a knife and chopped the things head off, where it started seeping black ooze. It bubbled and ran across the street before the creature itself turned to mist. Then another couple of them appeared out of nowhere. Pulling out a gun, he shot them some in the leg and shoulders and black ooze poured out of them all and he took of running away from the morbid scene.

"Nice." Marcus said, mostly to himself. He enjoyed shows like this, they were fast-paced and the guy always stopped the demons by the end of it. He couldn't recall what this particular show was called though and just settled in to a night of watching gunfire and someone fighting supernatural beings – hoping that eventually he'd pass out from exhaustion.

"Marcus, trust me. Your parents are lying to you... Maybe they're not really your parents..." Something whispered to him – trying to capture his attention.

He sat up, more alert this time as fear started to settle in and looked around again, trying to identify where the voice had come from, but again he could find nothing or nobody that could have uttered the words that appeared so close.

This had been happening too much – he was a normal kid, but this was weird. He decided, on a whim, to trust the voice and go listen to his parents, something he had never done before.

Although he was tired, Marcus knew the house like the back of his hand. He knew where it squeaked, where the cracks in the floors were and he knew how to sneak in and out of the house like a ghost. If he was going to go spy on his parents, they would never guess that he was there.

Listening carefully, Marcus lingered near his bedroom door. *Do I really want to do this? I am tired after all... I've barely slept a wink of sleep and I'm probably a bit drained from the events of the last few days.* He thought to himself.

The thoughts quickly ebbed away as he could hear the blare of the downstairs television. He decided, perhaps that it wouldn't hurt to go listen in and very carefully Marcus opened his bedroom door and snuck along the hallway. Creeping down the stairs, he snuck over to where the lounge was and waited near the door outside, listening intently to see if his parents would say anything.

"That's right, listen. Trust me." The voice said, before slipping away into nothingness; as if it was never there.

The voice irked Marcus, yet he trusted himself that he should listen to what has parents would say. He had a feeling after he left the study earlier that there was probably more that wasn't said – and they'd seen how tired he was so had decided to dismiss him as a result of it.

Peeking through the crack in the doorframe, Marcus watched as his parents gazed at each other as they spoke, the television flickering in the background, blazing loud enough so that Marcus could hear it from his bedroom upstairs.

"You know he's just doing what's right for his friends..." His mother said, picking at her dress and sighing.

"Yes, but he's... he's... been violent! It's so unlike him. Why is he doing something like this? He should know better and to use his words." His father retorted, scoffing.

"He's a kid, and he did look remorseful after we spoke to him."

"Yes, well he's going to end up throwing away his future if he's not careful. He should know better than to hang around gays and kids with broken home lives. We can't protect everyone, but we can protect ourselves. It's a lesson he'll need to learn at some point." His father said, crossing his arms defiantly.

Marcus drew away, not wishing to know more and feeling a sense of despair hanging in his chest. He was right – the voice was right – his parents had been lying about how they really felt about the situation.

"I told you..." The strange voice slid back, prickling Marcus' ears as it spoke, as if the person speaking was inches away from him. He felt a shiver run down his spine and tried to repel the unnerving feeling and bile that was rising in his throat.

Marcus drew back from the lounge and turned as if he was going to head back upstairs, not wishing to hear any more of his parents conversation. In fact, part of him was disgusted with himself for believing his parents had his best interests at heart; this was clearly not the case given their conversation – they'd felt the exact opposite of what they told him and had lied straight to his face. *Why weren't they honest with me on how I really felt?* He thought, feeling a horrible pain in his chest.

Yet, as he went to turn, he couldn't help himself, a part of him wanted to look at his parents and listen to just a bit more, to see if maybe they were wrong – and would somehow redeem themselves any moment.

So, he continued to watch them closely, waiting for them to carry on their conversation. However, as his father went to adjust the collar of his shirt, the man's eyes glimmered a dark shade of black.

Terrified he stepped back and turned immediately.

"Nope." Marcus whispered and quickly retreated back to his room.

Shutting the door quietly, he tired to breathe evenly through his nose, but couldn't help himself – the days events were just too much for him. He curled up in a ball on his bed and ran a hand through his hair. Turning the television set up, he watched the show with a lot more focus, as a mounting horror started to build up inside of him.

*

Marcus had watched the show intently for the last two weeks, in a way he had become obsessed. He'd barely slept and watched the show with a sense of urgency, needing answers.

He'd jotted down and done graphic drawings of all the creatures the supernatural television show depicted, and he'd watched interviews with the author and all the cast members – determined to figure out the secrets behind it and how it had somehow wormed it's way into his life.

A part of him wondered if maybe he was going crazy – after all he hadn't had a good nights sleep in weeks. Yet, none of it made sense. The whispers, his parents lying to his face, that dark glimmer he saw... *None of it makes sense... There has to be an explanation. It can't be a coincidence that I saw this show and then the same thing happened. I was meant to see it.* He thought to himself, as he continued to watch the television show.

The author had said he'd based the creatures and ideas off of real demons and myths that he had read about; apparently a fan of the occult. From that, Marcus had sorted all the creatures – if his parents were truly possessed/had been replaced with imposters – and the other things into sections.

There were the "imposters" which was the main part of the show, which he said was based on shapeshifters, which appears everywhere in mythology. Then he had said that there were other creatures, that he'd based certain things off.

There were "shadow creatures" which many people had reported seeing and had grown frightened of and then there were the hell hounds, which were basically dogs that snarled and growled, following you around and much larger than the average dog.

Yet, nothing explained the strange voice he had been hearing. In the show, the character didn't have a voice to guide him on how to avoid strange creatures. He had no idea what the voice may have been – or why it kept whispering to him rather than talking him.

Could it be something trying to lead him astray and replace him as well? Another imposter waiting to take away Marcus' life? The thought chilled him to the core and he could barely bare to stomach the idea of it. That something was trying to lure him to his death.

However, after various searches, he had come to his own conclusion. The whispers never felt bad, in fact it had guided him to the truth. Not to mention, that it had been trying to talk to him for awhile – it almost felt comforting in a way, as if it was his own voice talking to him.

No, he wasn't frightened of the whispers and so it had led him to believe that some kind of saintly spirit, or an angel was talking to him to keep him out of harms way, and that is why it had also started whispering to him before he got into a fight with George. To Marcus it all seemed to fit together as if he had just snapped in place the pieces of a puzzle – he was certain that he knew what was really going on with everything.

By the time he went back to school, everyone was concerned with him, but Marcus was going to keep his distance; he knew better than to engage with such people that could be imposters and he wasn't about to risk his life in case they had a plan to get rid of him as well... His father was right; he had to protect himself first and he wasn't going to risk getting killed when he was the only person that saw the truth; he needed to do what was right – and at the moment that was figuring out what these things wanted and how to get rid of them and who was safe.

Tyler, Maury and Jerimiah all came up to him on his first day back, trying to engage with him; but Marcus was having none of it. He kept to himself and shrugged them all off; each time they all looked hurt but shrugged, feeling that he may need space after the ordeal.

However, Marcus interpreted this very differently. His friends weren't very attentive and everyone seemed to be avoiding him at school. So he steadily came to the conclusion that they must be imposters as well. It bottled up inside of him sadly, when he realized that his best friend and his other friends were gone forever.

Yet, when the school bell rang his concerns quickly vanished as a crowd gathered in the hallway and some people began shrieking and cheering. Marcus made his way steadily through the crowd as everyone slowly dispersed and he realized that police officers had flooded the school. Alexi was being escorted out in handcuffs, winking and blowing kisses to everyone, looking like she had just won some kind of awards ceremony.

In fact, she looked like she was totally unphased by the police officers – almost as if she was hoping for something like this to happen. Her eyes seemed to glimmer hungrily at the attention she was lapping up, as the police officers tugged her forcefully and led her out of the school. Marcus watched confused at the ordeal and wondered what on earth had gone on. People started whispering around him, but it was difficult to make out what people were actually saying given how crowded the hallway was as Alexi disappeared out of sight of the long, colorful school hallways and towards the exit.

Eventually, Marcus couldn't resist. Maybe this had something to do with the strange things that he was seeing? It certainly, again, felt like a strange coincidence. Eventually, it was hard not to ask, so he made his way over to Maury – despite shrugging the boy off earlier in the day.

"What happened?" Marcus asked, hoping that if Maury was an imposter, he wouldn't suspect anything that Marcus had asked about his sister. In fact Maury – or what Marcus believed to be imposter Maury – didn't even look Marcus' way as he watched his sister.

Maury, in fact, looked embarrassed and like he wanted the ground to eat him up as he watched his older sister get escorted out of the school building and gates into a police cruiser.

Maury does often have to clean up after his sister's messes... This isn't exactly new behavior for him to act embarrassed. Then again, isn't this exactly what an imposter would do? They'd act like the person they're pretending to be to mislead everyone thinking that they're really them... Marcus through to himself.

Maury dragged a hand over his face, as if hoping his hands would scrub away the image. Marcus suspected that he thought if his reputation was difficult to manage now, it would be worse that his sister had been arrested again.

"You really don't want to know. Guess I'll be bailing her out tonight since mom and dad are on another vacation." He said miserably, as his sister disappeared from the school. With that Maury slithered into the crowd, hoping that people wouldn't look his way.

Yet Marcus felt this was odd – and further confirmed his theory. *After all, wouldn't he want to look after his family? Make sure any rumors are put to rest? Make sure that everyone knew the truth?* He thought to himself.

"Find out what happened." Something whispered to Marcus, the voice dark, seductive and as if it was trying to lure him somewhere.

Marcus looked around to see where the voice had come from, but there was nothing and he again felt the creeping horror building in his stomach that he had felt when he saw his father's eyes glimmer with darkness.

Then, Marcus really thought about it all and listened closely.

"Find out... All will be revealed..." It whispered and with that, he had realized that it was *the* voice, that had warned him about his parents and that had been whispering to him days prior – it was the same one and he had to follow what it said.

It was right. He needed to figure out the truth and then wherever this voice was coming from; hopefully it would reveal more to him. He had to trust that much.

But how? How do I find out? It won't exactly be easy to figure out... Especially given how I've reached to the imposters... I need to go to someone I trust... Someone that I know wouldn't be taken... He thought to himself; trying to figure out what to do next.

Biting his lip, he thought to how his parents – well what were pretending to be his parents – knew so much about George. Maybe, they would know the same about Alexi... Yet, he did he want to risk it?

Marcus was lucky the things hadn't caught him spying the other day. If he asked more about his classmates and explained what else had happened, they might suspect that he knew they knew far too much about his school...

No, he would need to talk to someone else. Someone that was close to Alexi... Marianne. She was quite close with Alexi and she trusted him.

Oh god, I hope those imposters didn't replace Marianne... Marcus suddenly thought with a pang. He'd always wanted to be with her, for as long as he could remember, and if she had been taken by one of those imposters, he realized that he would never get a chance to be with her.

"Talk to her... Find out..." A strange, hushed voice whispered and Marcus nodded to himself, pushing through the crowds which were still watching agape at the open door that Alexi had just been carted through.

Sure enough, after a bit of searching he spotted Marianne's slick, long ponytail and made his way over to her. She looked just as radiant as always, although at present her face awash with fear and concern for her friend.

Marcus stared at her for a moment, debating if he actually dared to find out if she was an imposter or not. A part of him wasn't sure if he'd be able to take it if she was... He'd never get the chance to ask her to the formal, to have that dance and ask her to be his girlfriend.

The plan that he had thought of days ago seemed almost ridiculous now. It felt like that idea and when he had been first watching her in the classroom was months and months ago, rather than just a few weeks. He remembered the way she smiled at him, as her ponytail had swished from side to side and watched her sadly for a moment.

I have to know the truth. That's better than not knowing. If she's not an imposter, then maybe there's hope for everyone. Maybe things will be alright. With that, Marcus managed to swallow his fear and strode over to her.

"You doing okay?" He asked delicately, watching her for any kind of sign that it wasn't his Marianne, but someone else that had tried to replace her.

"I'm... A bit all over the place really, especially with what just happened. What about you? You've been off for two weeks! It was so brave of you to stand up for Maury." She said, smiling up at him.

Her mascara was blotted beneath either one of her eyes and it looked like she had been crying. Marcus wanted nothing more than to bundle her up in his arms and stroke her hair, telling her everything would be alright.

Marcus blushed at the thought, suddenly feeling a bit more like his old self – the popular, carefree guy that all the girls in school fell over him for – the same one that was after Marianne's heart and would do whatever he could to try and win her over.

"What exactly happened? It looks like I missed a lot..." He said, gesturing to the crowd as the principal came along to try and break everyone up and urge them to go to their classes. His stony, stern expression seemed to wash over the crowd like a grenade and everyone quickly started dispersing and pushing past to get to their next class.

"Well... As you stuck up for her brother, I'll tell you it in confidence. You *cannot* tell anyone else though, you promise?" She said, looking up at him, her eyes going wide and pupil's dilating.

Marcus froze. Would his Marianne really divulge a secret of her best friend? He couldn't talk for a moment, finding himself speechless as he weighed up the possibility that she may not in fact be the girl that he had grown up with.

It was clear that Marianne had been holding in whatever the secret was for awhile, as she looked very distressed and like she was almost going to burst. Shifting her weight from foot to foot, and wiping her eyes delicately she took a deep breath as the load from her shoulders seemed to disappear, the words tumbling out of her mouth as if she was struggling to hold them in any longer.

"Well... She had taken some explicit videos with one of the guys a year younger than her – a junior actually. He counts as a minor. He circulated the video around school when you were off and she's been arrested for having sex with a minor and pornographic content with a child.

It's pretty stupid if you ask me, there's only a year between them and that idiotic boy is the one that circulated the video, but you know things are pretty messed up in this school – after all you got booted out for defending Maury." She said, hugging her arms tight and sighing sadly.

Marcus stared at her and pulled her into a hug knowing that she needed affection, but it was in that moment he knew something – that his Marianne was long gone and he would never see her again.

The Marianne he knew would surely never tell her friends secrets, especially to him. *And she wouldn't be relieved from it. In fact, she would be more worried that she had shared her best friends secret... Yet this isn't my Marianne. This is something else or someone else pretending to be her.*

He was more certain than ever that like everyone else she had been replaced with an imposter; the evidence of this was now clear as day in front of him. Yet without her and his parents, he felt something well up inside of him and it pained him right to his core.

He felt like there was no reason to go on. After all; everything in the last few weeks had been ripped away from him – and now knowing that the last piece of light that he had in his life was gone was just too much to possibly bear.

He was being watched by the teachers more closely since he had been suspended, he couldn't focus on math as well as before, he had fallen out with his best friend (and didn't really have the heart to make it up; especially as his best friend was gone forever and all that remained was something that was never his best friend in the first place), his parents had been taken from him and now, the only girl that he had ever had a crush on clearly had as well. It was sickening and spiraled through Marcus' body. He felt like a huge weight had been dumped on him and was almost impossible to carry.

After the crowd had started dispersing, Marianne slowly retreated from the hug and Marcus let go sadly, knowing that his Marianne was well and truly gone forever.

I have nothing. He thought as she slowly let go of him.

"Thanks Marcus, I really needed that. See you later... Text me sometime yeah?" She said, smiling sweetly at him before disappearing into the crowd and going to her next class.

Marianne would never ask that... She wouldn't want to text me. That isn't her. In fact, she rarely texts me outside of school hours unless it isn't about homework. I missed my chance to be with her. She's gone...

"You're right." Marcus almost jumped out of his skin as he saw someone leaning against the row of metal lockers beside him.

It was the guy from the television show that Marcus had been watching for the last few days. He stared in shock at the man, wondering if he was going to disappear in a cloud of smoke and almost as if he didn't really believe his own eyes.

This was too much; none of it made sense to Marcus. *Why is this happening to me? This doesn't feel real...*

"No, no way, you're not really here..." Marcus muttered, going to his locker and opening it up, trying to look away from what his eyes were seeing. He was almost certain that it was some kind of trick.

Yet, he was certain that everyone around him was acting differently. *The dark glimmer. His friends. Marianne...* He then went back to look at the man for a moment, wondering if he would disappear as soon as Marcus looked away, yet the character remained firmly placed in front of him, in fact he looked annoyed as if Marcus was wasting his time to refuse to believe his presence.

"If I'm not here why can you see me?" Colin asked, cocking an eyebrow at Marcus, daring him to give some kind of response back.

Yet Marcus found that he couldn't – he didn't have any explanation on why this was happening. He couldn't piece together any of it and everything just seemed to be rapidly spiraling out of his understanding and control.

He was dressed in a long, leather jacket and had sunglasses on his head. His hair was jet black and spiked up and he watched Marcus with a flat, bored look – as if even talking to him was a strain.

Underneath the long, leather jacket that trailed to his ankles, he wore a black shirt and dark jeans that hung on him smartly; just like in the television show. In fact, he looked like he'd walked straight out of the television and into the school hallway. Marcus blinked at the man a few times, expecting him to disappear, but instead he remained stood there, giving Marcus a defiant stare.

"You're an actor, you're called Charles Smith. There's no way you can be here." Marcus retorted quietly, as the halls started to empty and everyone hurried along to their classes.

"You know that you're wrong. You know that I'm here and you know that things aren't normal around here." He said back. Just like in the show, Colin looked like he was trying to hold back a laugh -as if he could believe how willfully ignorant someone was being around a matter of life and death.

All of a sudden, as he clenched his fists trying hard to ignore the man, Marcus realized that the hallway was empty and that he was running late for class. He looked around the quotes dispersed in the hallways and then back at Colin, who was staring at him with the same annoyed, bored look.

Marcus had enough and he just wanted to go. In fact, he didn't even want to go to class – he wanted to go home and shut himself in his room and pretend this was not happening. However, for now he would have to play it cool – he wasn't going to let anyone catch on with what he knew, or what he was thinking of doing. Sighing he got his books out of his locker and went to turn to head to class.

Yet, as he turned, he was stopped by a large, shadowy creature. He fell back in a alarm and went to shriek, but found that his breath was caught – he was frozen in terror, unable to speak or move. Watching the tall, shadowy creature advance towards him; yet he was frozen to the ground; trapped in place.

Colin flipped in front of Marcus – just like he often did in the show, brandishing a sword and sliced the strange creature in two, leaving it to become nothing more than smoke, which disappeared in the air.

"I have to go. You know I'm here. Call me when you're ready." He said and with that, he turned and walked around Marcus. He turned to watch him go, but the man was gone and Colin felt his heart hammer in his chest as he tried to process what had just happened.

Marcus looked around, feeling terrified and realized it was just him, alone, late for class and sitting in the hallway as he tried to gather his thoughts.

What the hell is going on? How did he do that? Was that really real? Did I just see that? How did he know a sword would work?

Thoughts swam through Marcus' head at a million miles per hour and he breathed evenly for a moment. *It doesn't matter. I just need to get through the day.* He thought to himself, gathering his things and rushing to the next class, ready to be surrounded with imposters whilst pretending he suspected nothing of the sort.

*

Alternative Universities and Realities by Prof. S. A.

Marcus sat, scrolling through the article on his computer with many other tabs open. Some people and scientists had mentioned that they thought that there were parallel universes to this one, and there were infinite realities. Marcus dived into a bit of a rabbit hole as he started scanning articles, books, theories, videos and other such things online.

He found a lot of them fascinating to read and realized, upon looking outside he'd been sat in front of the screen almost all afternoon and evening after school. The night was pouring in from his open window and a gentle breeze ruffled his grey, long curtains.

Standing up, Marcus stretched, letting his arms tower up as he heard his back crack – no doubt from being hunched over for so long. He went over to the windows and shut it and then drew the curtains closed, a bit shocked from how much time had passed and how quickly the day had ran by.

He turned his attention, once the window was firmly closed and the curtains drawn, to the article he was reading. This particular professor, mentioned that he believed that there were an unlimited number of infinite realities, pouring into one another and spiraling more and more out of control each day.

Yet, in particular, they also mentioned that because there were infinite realities, it meant that there were ones that fictional worlds were real; almost as if the worlds that authors created were bleeding from one reality into another; that authors, filmmakers and people who made television shows never really had true ideas and it was a way of one reality to bleed into another one. If fictional worlds could be real in one reality, then that meant that the imposters that Colin fought really had the possibility of coming to this one. Not to mention, the shadow creature that Marcus had seen... He leaned back in his chair thoughtfully, trying to piece it altogether, before looking up if there was any way to jump between universes or realities.

Instead of anything remotely scientific, a lot of sci-fi television shows flashed up instead alongside a list of books to buy. Marcus ran his hands over his face in frustration and sighed. Maybe, this reality meant that nobody believe it was a possibility and as such they couldn't dip from one to another; that made more sense then anything else he could think of and it certainly explained everything that Colin had seen so far.

After all, none of his friends were acting like his friends, everyone was acting strange and the world no longer seemed to fit together. In fact, Marcus today had been terrified, his eyes witnessing something that he still couldn't believe was fully real. The shadow had towered over him and Marcus had felt a terror rise in him that he'd never felt before. Even when he faced George to fight a few weeks ago, he hadn't felt anywhere near as scared as he had today.

He thought back to that moment where the huge shadow creature lurked over him and he had been frozen to the spot, helpless and terrified. It was an awful feeling, knowing that he was stuck and there was nothing he could do.

Yet, slowly he started again turning his mind to everyone else that he had seen over the last few days. He was certain that everyone around him was imposters and that other creatures had come here to take over everything... After all, it was the only logical explanation he could think of, and explained why Colin had turned up, why he saw the shadow and why he had heard the whispers. It all made sense... Yet there were still some things he was unsure of.

Deciding to go for a walk, Marcus gathered his things, pulling on a hoodie over his school uniform due to the breeze that had rippled through his window earlier and then pulled on some trainers that were resting at the bottom of his bed. Reluctantly, he stretched out again and then trudged down the stairs and out of the house, taking care to close the door so that his parents wouldn't notice that he slipped out. Although, he realized that he could hear his parents whispering nearby – probably in the lounge, but he didn't care.

I don't need to listen to what they have to say about me or what they think. I know enough already based on what I overheard last time and I certainly don't need to hear anything like that again. He thought bitterly.

He trudged out over the front lawn and started going for a walk, soaking in the cool, fall air. Taking a walk at night during fall was very different than the summer, the air itself seemed to be colder, more peaceful and more enticing than during the summertime. People were often more reluctant to brave the streets as well during the cold – as the people of Columbus seemed to thrive more in the summertime.

Oftentimes, Marcus felt like an outcast because of it as he walked through the quiet city and feeling the breeze brush against his face. He relished quietly as the leaves crunched beneath his feet softly and he advanced through the night deeper into the heart of the city itself.

He strode along the side walk, watching the busy city hum away – vibrant and full of life; which Marcus presumed was blissful ignorance. Although, it was never quite as busy as during the summer moths, life still went on and buses, cars and bikes went down the main rode. Marcus looked ahead of him, where he saw the city lights gleaming and decided he'd walk until his feet got tired and then just turn around and go back home.

Then, he saw a motorbike screech past him as he was walking down the street. The bike was red and had a large, picture of a dragon spattered across it. It seemed to screech and roar almost as it zipped in and out of traffic and out of sight with a sense of urgency.

Marcus froze in place. He knew that motorbike and seeing it caused the same sense of terror he had felt earlier in the day to rise up inside of him. He clenched at his chest in horror and stepped back.

"No..." He muttered, his heart hammering in his chest, against his hand. He turned around, striding fast and quickly. Needing to get home – not wishing to see it – but it was too late.

Sure enough, whipping after it was Colin's famous motorbike as well. Marcus felt like he was going crazy.

The motorbike was pretty obvious to spot and was very well-known as Colin's. The bike itself was silver and seemed to shimmer against the light as it darted through traffic. Of course, it helped that Colin never wore a motorbike helmet and just as he sped past, he caught Marcus' eye and winked. Marcus, aghast and startled could only look on as Colin chased after the other bike.

How was he seeing these things and nobody else was? Yet as he watched Colin's motorbike disappear into the night, he knew that nobody else seemed to understand or recognize that something seemed amiss – but of course, Marcus already knew the answer. Everyone around him was imposters and they couldn't see what was going on, or they could and they chose to act normal so that Colin wouldn't hunt them down as well.

In the show, around the sixth season, there was a dark, dangerous demon that could flip into new realities and it took on the form of a young woman and a motorbike. She could actually transform into a dragon and could easily torch an entire city if she wanted too. Marcus scolded himself for not thinking that this could be the reason he'd been seeing everything he had been sooner. It all made sense after all; he was seeing Colin, the shadows – why wouldn't it be something like that.

Yet, it didn't make sense in this world. The author himself had said that he made the demon up because he couldn't find anything like it in any kind of occult book or demonology one that he had studied.

But... a scientist mentioned in one of those articles that they believe authors have the ability to see into other worlds. It bleeds into ours, through the works of fiction such as books, television shows... Marcus clasped his arms as the thoughts rocked his mind.

It was too much for Marcus, he ran back home, yet opened the door quietly, still not wishing to alert his parents to everything he knew. The house was silent as he stepped through the hallway and trudged upstairs defeatedly.

Swinging open his bedroom door, he shut it again quietly and took off his hoodie and shoes, setting them down neatly before opening the curtains and staring into the night. In that moment, something broke inside of him. He was already defeated, given everything that had gone on over the last couple of weeks, but this was just too much, like something had snapped and had tipped him over the edge.

I can't live in a world like this.

~ 5 ~

THE EMERGENCY

"It's my experience that people are a lot more sympathetic if they can see you hurting, and for the millionth time in my life I wish for measles or smallpox or some other easily understood disease just to make it easier on me and also on them." —*Jennifer Niven*

Marcus stayed in his room, again ignoring his parents requests for them to join them for dinner – he had no intention of sitting and eating with imposters. They could poison his food, they could hurt him or worst of all; maybe they suspected that Colin had visited him and was going to do something about them.

He didn't want to give them that satisfaction and wanted to do things on his own terms, no matter what. So, Marcus had just mentioned that he ate a lot at school and wasn't feeling particularly hungry when his parents had pestered him about eating more, becoming healthy and strong for soccer practice and this and that. Yet, with how insistent Marcus was, they understood that he was probably eating enough and was old enough to recognize when he was full.

To Marcus however, the situation just seemed odd in itself, his parents – first and foremost – were concerned with his wellbeing. Yet, being imposters; they of course didn't pry or check any further on him, in fact Marcus found it bizarre that they had started leaving him more and more to his own devices following the fight and suspension he had faced.

Slowly, Marcus realized they didn't doubt him for so much as a second that he knew the truth either; about what they really were and what they were hiding from him. There was also the fact that because of that, they didn't suspect a single thing on what Marcus was actually planning to do about all of this.

He waited and listened for everyone to retreat to bed and it was then that he knew what he had to do. He breathed deeply as he came to terms with what he needed to do to rid himself of all of this. He was just about to sneak downstairs to his fathers study, when his phone flashed up.

Sighing, he want to pick it up and looked at it, surprised to see a name that hadn't texted him for a good few days pop up.

Marcus! Help! It's Alexi, I don't know who else to call.

She may be an imposter, but she was an imposter of his Marianne; he still cared about her, even if it wasn't really her and he wasn't going to let whatever happened ruin their lives. After all, in the show, Colin had found the originally people that the imposters were of and some of them had got along with their duplicates – in fact, they'd even stuck together, some of them finding comfort in the fact that they had someone that understood them completely.

It didn't end that way for all of them though; most of the imposters became imposters as they ate the people they were attempting to be and then took over their lives. They wanted to literally make their life their own; in a twisted and dark way – which is where Colin came in.

Should I really help her if it's not my Marianne? What would the real Marianne want me to do...? If it's an imposter though, she's based off the real Marianne and if she doesn't know what to do she must really need my help as I'm the only one she's texted. Marcus thought, biting his lip.

Sighing as he decidedly made up his mind, he threw on his hoodie and laced up his trainers and so instead of sneaking downstairs to go to his father's study, he snuck downstairs to the hall-way, before sneaking out of the door.

It was almost ridiculous how easy it was to sneak out of his parents house. He wondered if they knew. They had caught him a few times before; but it felt like they didn't care anymore.

Like they are someone else and not themselves. Marcus thought to himself sadly. He wondered if maybe they had been replaced with imposters much sooner and he didn't realize; which then led to his thoughts spiraling as he walked down the steps and across their front lawn.

The city was almost silent as he snuck outside; it was far, far later than Marcus was used to going out and although Columbus was big, it was rare that it was buzzing when it was this early in the morning or late at night. People in the buzzing city really liked their sleep and as such, you could almost hear a pin drop if you listened carefully enough.

The moon hung in the sky, but the clouds were pouring over the stars; as if the sky agreed that the world had changed and it didn't wish to shine a harsh light on the situation. Although with the streetlights, it wasn't difficult to see – which Marcus was thankful for as he went to untie his bike from the bike chain that was slung across it, nearby the family cars.

Marcus hopped on the slick, red bike his parents had got him for his 15th birthday and started pedaling into the night. Figuring that if he was planning on putting an end to all this nonsense, he might as well help someone... or *something* out before he did.

*

Alexi was keeled over, vomit was dribbling from the sides of her mouth when Marcus arrived. She was curled up in a ball and was wearing nothing but a bralette and a skirt that seemed to have been hitched up and caught in her underwear.

The field she was laid in was far from the city itself and was in a part that Marcus had never even been to before. In fact, he felt dread creep up inside of him as he pedaled into the night and took up the twists and turns towards it. Seeing the girl, laid in the grass and unconscious of the huge, field however made Marcus feel uncomfortable. The timing didn't help matters either, the clouds still seemed to pour, not giving much light onto the situation, yet from some streetlights flickered on the road opposite he could see just how rough Alexi looked.

She looked terrible, her skin was so pale it was almost see-through and her face looked green, almost blue. Her ribs were protruding from her skin and her hair was full of sticks and twigs. Her chest rose and fell softly, but with a strain as if it was difficult breathing – or if she was about to vomit again.

Marcus ditched his bike and took his hoodie off, putting it around her shoulders, as upon closer inspection he also noticed that she was shivering.

I won't need that hoodie soon anyway, I guess it doesn't matter if she has it and it keeps her at least a little bit warm for awhile. He thought to himself.

Slowly, he rolled the girl into the recovery position and stepped back, his eyes glaring and dark as he stared at Marianne. Not wanting to assume that she could hurt her – yet as an imposter there was no limit on what she was capable of.

Well... If she's Marianne's imposter, she shares the same thoughts, feelings and knowledge as Marianne does. So surely she wouldn't hurt her friend? In fact, she'd want to turn Alexi into an imposter as well, and this isn't the way it's done. No, she couldn't of hurt Alexi. Something else must have gone on... Marcus thought to himself as his eyes narrowed at her.

"What happened?" he asked her, trying hard not to sound suspicious or demanding as Marianne stared at Alexi, who appeared to be breathing in a much lighter and easier way now that she was in a safer position.

Marcus watched her carefully, ready to grab Alexi if he needed to and set off running. He wasn't particularly sure though, how far he would get or what he would do next. After all, they were far, far away from the hubbub of the city and were in a strange, large field that Marcus himself had never even ventured by before. Then he noticed that Marianne's face was damp with tears and she was shuddering as she watched her friend. Almost like she was terrified that Alexi would be lost to her.

Well, imposters do have memories of the person they're impersonating. It makes sense she'd be upset... It's a bit like the show she put on the other day when Alexi got escorted out of school in handcuffs. Her eyes were damp, she acted and looked a bit like my Marianne, but she isn't... Marcus thought to himself, awaiting Marianne to explain or say something more.

She watched for a moment, and then Marcus noticed just how differently the two girls were dressed. Marianne was dressed very differently to Alexi; almost as if they had been in completely different places before any of this had even happened. In fact, Marianne had looked as if she had just rolled out of bed. She was wearing pajamas and boots, but with a parka wrapped around her body, huddling into it as much as she could, as if the cold was going to cut through her very skin.

"She said she was going to party with some older boys, but I'd been noticing for a few days that she hadn't really been eating..."

With that, she gestured to the ribs that were sticking out of Alexi's skin on either side of her body, just underneath the little bralette that Alexi was wearing. Alexi coughed and some more vomit trickled out of her mouth, onto the grass beneath her and she seemed to coil up into Marcus' hoodie a bit more; as if subconsciously, she knew that she was now safe from whatever had happened and was with people that she could trust.

"...I was worried about her, that as she hadn't been eating much, she wasn't really in her best state of mind. So, I put a tracker in her phone.

I know I shouldn't have done it and it was an invasion of her privacy but I was... Worried. At first it looked fine, she was hanging out at a frat party further in the city, but then she was getting driven out here..."

Marianne gestured to the field that seemed to ripple endlessly into the darkness of the night. Her slim hands quivering as she gestured.

"I immediately got my parents car and followed the tracker, I saw some boys dragging her into the field and beeped at them.

They all ran off as soon as they saw the car and headlights... I didn't know what to do... She's been arrested so many times by the police, I don't think they'll listen or do anything if I take her to the station."

With that, it looked like Marianne couldn't hold it anymore and she burst into tears. The sobs were gasping, heaving and Marcus realized for the first time the girl could actually not look very pretty sometimes.

Watching her, he wasn't sure how to react – or for that matter even if he should react at all. It wasn't *his* Marianne that was acting this way, it was just something pretending to be her, to lure him in. Yet, he couldn't help but feel guilt begin to bubble away inside of him as he watched her. He felt awkward – he knew she wasn't a real person – but he didn't like seeing anyone cry.

I need to think. I don't want to deal with this, I can't deal with this. She's not my Marianne, it's not the Marianne I'll ever get to ask out, or hug, or kiss. It's not the Marianne I pictured asking to the formal, but I can't just leave her here to deal with this... Whether she's my Marianne or not, she's still some kind of Marianne and I need to help her. Marcus thought decidedly.

"Listen, let's get her somewhere quieter okay? I'm sure she'll be fine." He said, gently patting her on the back and trying to keep her at arms length.

He didn't particularly want to touch the girl again, following the sickening feeling he had the other day following he hug he had given her. He didn't want that drop in his stomach to come again, he had to keep her at arms length – for his own sake.

Marianne, however, oblivious to whatever Marcus was thinking managed to compose herself. Drawing herself back and taking some deep breaths, her sobs slowly muted into sniffs.

The boy watched her with a quiet fascination – he could never understand how girls could cry so much or so openly flaunt how they felt – imposter or not. It was like it was some universal language that everyone needed to know and understand how they felt – that it was okay to talk or cry or whatever else.

Yet, Marcus just felt awkward as had watched her cry and reel herself back in. He didn't really think crying could be as therapeutic as girls made it out to be and it looked almost horrifying. Spilling your guts out to the world as tears dribbled down your face.

No – I'd rather stab myself in the eyes with nails. He thought, trying hard not to show that he was thinking about how gross crying was in general.

Luckily, Marianne spoke, having collected herself.

"We cannot take her back to her place. Maury will be mortified and her parents get back from vacation tomorrow. If they find out, they will kill her." She said, staring at her friend with a terrified expression; empathetic to the potential situation Alexi's parents would no doubt unleash.

Marcus nodded, and picked up the girl with ease. Shockingly, he realized she was as light as a feather, her weight barely having any impact on holding her. Marianne was right, she clearly had not been eating much recently based on how light she felt.

He actually felt a bit ruffled holding her, he could feel the girls bones against his hands as he picked her up. A sense of guilt washed over him again – although, he knew that he couldn't help her. He couldn't really help anyone right now and he was doing this more for the actual Marianne's sake than anyone else. Almost like a final farewell to the person she would've been.

Carrying her, like a mother would carry an infant, he took the girl to Marianne's car and put her in the back seat. Fastening her in carefully and putting her in to the best of his ability the recovery position on the back seats, so that if she did end up vomiting again at all, she wouldn't choke on her own vomit in front of them.

"You got any bags?" He asked, turning to Marianne as he stood up.

Marianne nodded and went to the boot of the car where a load of grocery bags were sitting. They laid out the bottom of the car and carefully made sure that Alexi was strapped inside of the car safely.

"What do I do now...?" Marianne asked, watching her friend slump over. A look of defeat running across her face. She looked like she thought she was the worst friend in the world – like she should've spoken up or said something sooner.

I can't blame her for not calling the police... Or Maury... Maury looked like he was no help the other day in the school and the only thing he was worried about was his reputation and bailing her out. I don't blame her for coming to me... Maybe it's because she told me the reason why Alexi got arrested in the first place? Marcus thought, watching Marianne try hard to hold herself together.

She turned to look at him expectedly, hoping that Marcus had some kind of magical solution that would fix everything. He bit his lip for a moment and thought hard on what the next best steps could be, given Alexi's current state.

"Let's go to the nearest 24/7 diner okay? We'll get her cleaned up, try and wake her up and get some food in her. It should help." He said decidedly.

His mother and father had always said that the best hangover cure they could ever had was greasy food (plain if they were feeling sick) and lots of water. He presumed that it must be the same if you were quite drunk and figured the best place to get something like that was one of the many diners that were constantly open in the city.

Of course; he was certain that they would look at them like they were mad striding in so late at night/early in the morning to one –

but he couldn't think of any other options that would end in Alexi not getting in trouble with either her parents or the police with something that clearly wasn't her fault anyway.

Marianne seemed to think the plan over for a moment and then nodded and a wave of relief seemed to fall off her shoulders as she seemed to realize that she wasn't in this alone.

She gave one last look at her friend, slumped over and strapped in in the backseat, before getting up and going to open the drivers side door. Breathing deeply she leaned back closing her eyes for a moment, before putting the keys in the ignition.

Marcus hopped in the car, leaving his bike to the grassy fields. After all, he couldn't imagine needing it again after tonight and he was sure one of the many imposters lurking with in the city would probably love a new bike to cause more mayhem with. Either that or he pictured colin zipping along on his motorbike and ditching it to take up Marcus' little mountain bike.

The thought made him grin as Marianne put her car into reverse and they left the long stretch of field and grassland, going back into the city to where the throb of life still hummed.

The three of them sped to the diner in Marianne's car and Marcus was relieved to see streetlights, city lights and to be around more than two people again. Being in that field with just one or two people felt unnerving, strange even.

As Marianne pulled into the parking lot, Marcus got out of the car and headed inside once she was parked. Marcus had the good sense to bring his wallet and cards should they need anything – as he expected that whatever he was about to arrive too when he set off to find Alexi and Marianne it might not be pleasant and he may need cash, or cards to help them out.

There were some perks to being the rich kid in Columbus – granted there were not many when your life had been turned upside down by strange *things* but this was one of them. You could literally buy your way out of almost any situation and get whatever you needed, whenever you wanted.

He wished that there was some magic, money potion that could fix the imposters and the shadows that he had been seeing, but Marcus knew that there was no such thing and had resigned himself to the one and only plan that had made sense; since all the madness had begun.

The diner itself was named "Mabel's Diner" and was brightly lit. The place itself seemed to stick out like a sore thumb and the 24/7 sign buzzed on the outside of it. The place looked almost empty when the teenagers arrived but it looked like a stereotypical diner that was often found in television shows. Inside, it was covered in checked tablecloths and waitresses dressed in large, drab aprons and blue dresses.

The woman behind the counter looked bored and stared at the two teenagers with disinterest she steadily drank from a coffee cup that rested on her table, as if it was the only thing that was keeping her alive and functioning right now. Yet, her eyes seemed almost glazed over in a way, as if she had been downing shots all night. Marcus coughed, and she turned her attention to him dazedly. He bought some plain food for the unconscious girl and some greasy, hearty food for both him and Marianne.

They retreated back to Marianne's car once they had got the food and some drinks. A sense of relief flooded through him as he bit into a burger, whilst Marianne dashed to the toilet to get some tissues, water and soap to clean up Alexi. Marcus realized that he hadn't actually eaten very much in the last few days, and greasy meat felt amazing biting into.

The way the bread fell across his tongue, the crunch of the lettuce and how the cheese paired with the beef of the burger flooded sensations into his mouth. He just enjoyed and savored the first bite for a moment, then took a second and smiled to himself.

Suddenly, Marcus heard a familiar voice and he froze, putting the food down and sighed; almost as if he knew he wasn't allowed to enjoy anything for too long, before something else was going to interrupt him.

"You saw me chasing her earlier huh? Is that why you freaked out?" Colin asked, a playful and cunning smirk dancing on his lips. He was perched just next to Alexi's feet, as she was now curled up in a ball and sleeping, her face still up and overlooking the bags below the seat, should she suddenly begin vomiting again.

Colin looked almost comical in a way, with how out of place he looked in the small car. His leather coat seemed to not quite fit in with the surroundings and Marcus was almost certain it seemed to glimmer or flicker in the edges. Yet, Marcus knew, defeatedly, that he must be really here – after all, why else would he see him?

However, he was not willing to engage in this madness after the night he had, so Marcus turned his head, not willing to engage or entertain the strange man that had been following him since everything began to get uncertain in his life. In fact, he was more annoyed and sad that his appetite had now disappeared – as it was the first time in awhile that he had truly been enjoying his food – and it didn't feel like he was just eating for the sake of it.

He looked at the burger longingly as Colin climbed from the back seat into the drivers seat where Marianne had been sat and began staring at Marcus intently. Slowly, Colin advanced on Marcus, pointing his finger him and drawing closer; his face twisted into a look of disappointment and sheer disbelief.

"You know she's possessed right? Replaced? She's an imposter. She's not real. The girl you liked, the girl you loved is long, long gone. The only way to get rid of her is to cut off her head, forcefully I would add and with a butchers knife. You'll thank me when black ooze starts seeping out of that creature." Colin said demandingly and darkly; scowling at Marcus.

"I'm not going to do that. Possessed or not, she helped her." Marcus said, gesturing to Alexi, who was still slumped over. As if realizing that someone had spoken about her, even though she was unconscious she sniffed suddenly in her sleep before continuing to breath evenly and deeply.

Marcus watched her for a moment, wishing that he could do more. He never really liked Alexi that much. She was very handsy and tried it on with all the boys often; yet it was definitely hard having a brother that was out – it put a big target on your back.

Based on what Maury had said as well, their parents were absent often, leaving Alexi in charge; which Marcus couldn't help but presume was a very big responsibility to take on. He watched her, sadly – thinking of how difficult a life it must be for the young girl and almost as if he was really seeing her for the first time.

"Yeah, but she's evil. You need to get rid of her, you know that it's the right thing to do. You can see me for a reason – and there's something deep down in you that knows it too." Colin said, his voice patronizing as if he were talking to a child.

Marcus shook his head, he had a plan in place and Colin wasn't going to be able to sway him otherwise on what to do and so Colin shrugged as if he was starting to give up and understanding that Marcus didn't care and that he didn't have the willpower to fight back on.

Suddenly, the backdoor opened as Marianne climbed in to the car and started cleaning up her friend's face, gently wiping the vomit off it, and then listening carefully to her breathing, almost as if she was checking to see if her lungs still worked.

"I'm going to get a cup of cold water, to splash over her face." Marcus said flatly, trying to ignore how painful it was to see an imposter cleaning up after Marianne's best friend.

He was almost certain that Alexi wasn't an imposter, as Alexi had been acting exactly like she always did. In a way, Marcus felt almost bad; knowing that he'd be leaving her behind – but seeing how careful Marianne's imposter was and given the events of the night, he imagined that he was in fact leaving her in good hands that could look after her.

Marianne, too engulfed in trying to clear up her friend, nodded as Marcus headed back inside of the diner. He heard Colin's footsteps but he ignored him as he ordered a cup of ice water from inside of the diner.

The waitress watched him with a bored, exhausted look. Her eyes still glazed as he ordered the water. She poured it slowly from the tap and passed it to him, throwing some chunks of ice in there for good measure.

The entire woman's face was almost devoid of expression; as if even trying to look or act a certain way was too much effort and simply taking the orders was a strain. Marcus watched her for a moment before he instead looked down at the water and the ice floating in chunks in the plastic cup.

"You see! She's possessed too. Look at her! Her eyes are glazed, she's staring into space, barely responding. I bet if you look closely you can't even see a flicker of light in her eyes. It's all been destroyed and taken by darkness.

I know you're happy to see me in a way, I know that deep down you're glad that I'm here. You know you're not crazy and that I can help you, I can help rid this world of evil just like I did my own." Colin said, attempting to stand in front of Marcus and flailing his arms like a mad man.

Why can't he leave me alone? I know what I'm doing and I don't care what this guy thinks. He can save the world if he wants but I'm no hero. I can't live like this. I can't do this. I just want to go home. He thought, turning around.

Marcus was having none of the antics of this character. It was all just too overwhelming and he had no intention to pay attention to him. He thanked the zoned-out waitress for the water and exited the restaurant. Hearing the bell jingle as he left.

Colin slipped in front of him as Marcus walked towards the car. Eventually he stopped, and looked up at the sky, still hiding the stars with clouds – determined not to look at the man that was dancing around in front of him trying to get his attention.

"Stop ignoring me! What are you afraid of! You know I'm right!" Colin screamed, his coat flapping in the fall breeze.

For a moment, Marcus stopped and looked at him. He looked so powerful; it was no wonder that he had been selected to rid the world of the strange creatures that Marcus was sure his world had become infested with. Yet, he knew that they had chosen the wrong man for the job to help out.

He wasn't as powerful as Colin, nor was he as direct or confident. In a way, he was afraid and the things that he had seen made him realize that he lost everyone and that he didn't want to lose himself.

In the show, the only thing that Colin had to keep him sane, was his wife he helped get rid of the creatures with him. He'd eventually saved her from the dragon (the very same one he was chasing on the motorcycle earlier) and together they had killed what they thought was the last of the imposters.

Yet, the imposters had taken everyone that Marcus loved. He couldn't bare to be around anyone anymore. He was certain that someone would find the strength to stop the strange creatures yet it wasn't him.

"I don't care if you're right. I don't care if you're wrong. Just LEAVE ME ALONE!" Marcus screamed, and with that, Colin vanished into the night.

Marianne came jogging up from the car and looked around concerned.

"Are you okay? What's wrong? Was someone in the restaurant bothering you?" She asked delicately, wrapping her hands around his arm.

"I know what you are and what you did. I'm sick of pretending that I don't. Take this and sort her out. I'm going home."

"But it's like 2am! You left your bike in the field! Marcus, what do you mean? What is going on?!" Marianne said, looking hurt and her face a mess of concern.

"Nothing. Goodbye Marianne." He said, and with that he turned on her and stared walking away.

*

By the time he got home, his phone was blowing up with texts, but not just from Marianne. Jerimiah, Tyler and Maury had all texted him trying to figure out what was wrong.

Look man, we're best friends. Please talk to me, I care about you.

I'm not good at talking, but I'm good at listening. You can always talk to me.

Come on man, you saved me from George! The least I can do is help you figure this out, call me if you need someone yeah?

Marcus looked at them all, with a bored, sad expression and turned his phone off. He knew exactly what he needed to do now and there wasn't a doubt in his mind.

The house was quiet, and he knew that soon, he would be joining his real parents.

~ 6 ~

THE REVOLVER

"...we live in a world where if you break your arm, everyone runs over to sign your cast, but if you tell people you're depressed, everyone runs the other way. That's the stigma. We are so... accepting of any body part breaking down, other than our brains. And that's ignorance. That's pure ignorance. And that ignorance has created a world that doesn't under-stand depression, that doesn't understand mental health." — *Kevin Breel*

Marcus sat in his father's study looking at the Revolver that sat above the mantel piece. The shotgun glimmered at him, as if it knew what he was planning.

Slowly, he took the Revolver out of the case where it sat proudly, and began putting bullets into it. He remembered the very first time his father had explained to him how it worked, at the time they had gone to a gun range together.

His father was an author, of many drab, dull books but some of them were murder mysteries which revolved around weapons.

"You can always find out what kind of man someone is from the kind of gun they choose. People who use revolvers, they are tacti-cal, methodical – they plan what they want to do with it and the firing shot echoes far and wide, with everyone knowing you've shot something well.

It's a powerful gun." He said, grinning.

At the time, he'd slowly taught Marcus how to hold it, stand, look down the sights and shoot from it. His father had praised him following their time at the gun range, he'd hit target.

"A born shooter! You're a natural my boy!" He'd exclaimed.

Yet, today he didn't really care much, there was only one thing he needed to make sure he shot.

Once the gun was loaded, he slowly placed the revolver into his mouth. The cool metal gently passed his lips as he felt the gun slide across his tongue.

He'd never really considered what a gun would taste like, and now that would be the last thing, he ever presumed that he thought as his hand shuddered.

"MARCUS! WHAT ARE YOU DOING?! DROP THAT!" His mother exclaimed rushing into the study.

Slowly, he took the gun out of his mouth and stared at her sadly.

"You're not really my mother. I know what you are. Now go." Marcus said, his voice drained of air.

His mother, was undeterred however and rushed over to him, desperately trying to wrestle the gun out of his hands.

Marcus knew then, he had to find a way to end all this and pulled the trigger, just as his mother snatched the gun out of his hands.

"What have you done?!" Marcus' father said quietly, aghast as he rushed in the room and his mother remained curled up in a ball as blood gushed from her shoulder.

Blood. Marcus thought, before he fainted at the sight.

~ 7 ~

THE RECOVERY

There is so much pain in the world, and most of these people keep
theirs secret, rolling through agonizing lives in invisible wheelchairs,
dressed in invisible bodycasts." —Andrew Solomon

Marcus sat, terrified in the bed when a woman came to sit with
him. She had hair that was tied up in a bun and she had warm,
honey eyes. The clothes she wore, indicated that the room that
Marcus was in was some kind of hospital, but he had no idea what
kind of hospital he was in.

The walls were grey and stony – so it definitely didn't look like
a prison. He had a large window as well, although he noticed it appeared to be bolted shut – as if whoever was keeping him here was
concerned he'd try and escape.

He noticed that the window overlooked a long, open field where
there were a lot of people in similar, blue clothes to him striding
around. Some of them laughing, others crying and even some who
were drawing.

He turned his attention to the woman who was sat next to him,
trying hard to focus on where he was and what was going on. She
was wearing pink slacks and sat with him on the bed, smiling at
him softly. She had kind eyes, which made Marcus trust her, even
if he was scared.

"Is my mom okay?" He asked quietly.

"Yes, do you remember what happened?" She asked delicately.

"I remember the shooting, I don't remember what happened after... Next thing I remember is waking up here..." He said.

She nodded, before folding her hands into her lap.

"Well, after you passed out, your father called an ambulance, explained everything to us and we figured that you should come here for thirty days, to get some help.

Have you ever heard of schizophrenia?" She asked.

Marcus looked at her, his eyes wide with fear and shook his head slowly – aghast.

The nurse nodded slowly and put her hand on his shoulder.

"It's okay, it's not a death sentence. There is so much medicine and things around these days. In the USA it impacts 2.6 million people.

A lot of people actually don't manage to get help before it's took late. You're very lucky that your mother was there to help you." She said softly.

Marcus curled up into a ball on the edge of the bed. *No. I was popular. I had everything. How could I get schizophrenia?*

"But... Crazy people have that disease?! It's for people that are crazy, delusional..." He trailed off as everything slowly started to make sense.

The voice that he had heard whispering to him was the schizophrenia, so was Colin appearing.

"No... I can't be crazy..." He whispered, horrified and upset with himself.

"You're not crazy, I've been told that you're a very smart and kind kid. In fact, it seems to me that you were trying to hurt yourself, so that you wouldn't hurt anyone around you. Do you want to tell me more about what happened? What you saw?" She asked.

Marcus shook his head, trying to grapple with the fact that he had this... *disease.*

The nurse nodded and gently stroked his shoulder.

"All in your own time. There's a buzzer at the end of the bed. We're going to have a doctor come in, in a few days time to do an evaluation. It won't take as long if we have some notes regarding what you've been seeing, but again, take it all in your own time. You're safe here." She said.

With that, she left the room before giving him one last empathetic glance.

Once the door clicked shut, Marcus balled up in the metal, hard bed and thought of his room, with his own bed longingly. Then he thought of his television and all the shows he'd watched with criminals, or crazy people.

Half of the shows he'd ever watched in his entire life revolved around some crazy person with an illness like schizophrenia. It *must* be bad. He *must* be crazy. Why else would he be surrounded with things like that on a daily basis?

He was always taught that men shouldn't cry, but in that moment something inside of him snapped and he couldn't contain himself anymore. He began sobbing and tears began running down his cheeks as he realized that his life was well and truly ruined.

*

Marcus sat with the nurse. He'd been in the facility for seven days now, but he felt it was time to tell the truth about everything that he saw.

"Am I crazy? Literally in every single film, television show or book I've ever seen or read, anyone with an illness like mine is a bad guy..." Marcus said sadly, staring into the distance.

"It is very easy for media companies to make outlandish claims for illnesses they don't understand. Mental health is demonized in our culture so much, to the point that people look down on others with illnesses.

It actually causes a lot of issues for people in their day-to-day lives. People are less likely to seek out help, they feel guilty for suffering and like you many people think of ending it all because they think that all life has to offer them is pain.

Look around at everyone sat in here with us, every single one of them have felt that way at some point. Myself included." The nurse said, gesturing.

Sophie was the nurse that Marcus had spoken to on his first day in the facility and he felt like he could trust her. She had been nothing but kind to him during the first, scary few days and had been patient in waiting for him to open up and come to her first.

As requested, he looked around at the canteen to everyone that was sat eating, drinking or playing with their food. He noticed that quite a few of them had scars. One had a horrific scar around their neck... Which looked an awful lot like rope burn. There was a young girl sat several tables away who kept tugging the pajamas she was wearing in an attempt to cover her wrist that had huge, scarring slits running up and down them.

Slowly, it began to dawn on Marcus that the nurse was right. He thought steadily back to school and how Maury and Tyler were picked on a lot. Maury was a target, because he was different. He liked guys and there were a lot of people – teachers included – that didn't like that. It was brave of Maury to be he who was, even though the consequences were rained on him every day.

Then there was Tyler, who mostly kept to himself. Tyler was quiet, meek and shy – but he was who he was. He didn't change for anyone. Although, the teachers and people like George took it as a personal offence almost that he was quiet.

Sophie was right; the world hated people that were different and now that Marcus knew just how different he was, he knew it was going to be hard to fight the same battles those two boys did. He would be rolled up into a box and seen the same way as every-one else.

"Can you promise me, honestly that it gets better? That I won't just be put in a 'box' labelled 'crazy' my whole life? Because, it kind of feels like that is exactly what's going to happen to me. Who would give a job to someone with a mental health issue? How will I get into college? Will I even still get a scholarship?

I'm worried that now I'm starting to accept I have this... *thing*... It will make me stand out like a sore thumb. I'll have a big target on the rest of my life, a stamp on my head that says I'm worthless." He said, playing with his hands and refusing to look up at Sophie, just in case she had that look of pity in her eyes.

"You're not worthless. If anything you're a hero. You're fighting a battle that many other people can't see. Some things are going to be harder because of it, but you have such a bright future ahead of you. I know it.

I struggled with depression and anxiety as a teenager. I tried to end my life and I'm glad that it failed. Today, I can be here, with kids like you and help them see their worth." She said kindly, grabbing his fidgeting hands softly.

Suddenly, it felt like a weight was lifted off his shoulders. If she had tried to kill herself, if she had mental illnesses and could now help others with them, it meant there was hope for Marcus and that he wasn't doomed.

"So, are you going to tell me more about what happened, the things you saw?" She said, letting go of his hands gently and grabbing a notebook and pen.

Taking a deep breath, he started telling her about his story.

~ 8 ~

A FRESH START

"Nothing diminishes anxiety faster than action." — *Walter Anderson*

Marcus paced throughout his room nervously. The doctor had diagnosed him with schizophrenia and he had started taking medication. The hallucinations had stopped whilst he'd been in the facility most of the time, other than the occasional whisper that he'd hear. However, he had learnt from experience and reported it every time to the nurse who would note it down.

From everything that he had told Sophie, they were able to fast-track the diagnosis with the Doctor, which also meant he was able to get medicated quicker to stop the hallucinations. They Doctor had also recommended therapy for Marcus as well, but he mentioned that Marcus should start it when he was discharged.

He had now been in the facility for almost fifteen days, but today he was nervous for a different reason. Today was the first day that he was seeing his parents since he had been sent here.

In a way, it had been easier for him to open up to the nurse and get a grip on his surroundings. His false reality had melted away without seeing them. A part of him though was worried, he'd got obsessed that they were imposters - although through talking with the Doctor and Sophie, he knew that it was actually part of the schizophrenia that was making him see things, believing that they were false.

In fact, they had mentioned that the conversation he overheard where it all started may have even been a hallucination at the time. A part of him doubted it, he knew his parents well enough to know that if they were going to talk about him they'd at least presume he was out of earshot, and their house was big enough that if he was in his room, he'd of never have heard their conversation.

"They're here." Said Sophie, coming to his door.

He nodded and flattened down the clothes he was wearing before walking with her. His feet made a padding sound, as they made their way through the mental health hospital and to the visitation room.

Both of his parents were sat at a table in the visiting area, right next to the vending machine. He noticed, with a pang, that his mother was wearing a large blazer, but it was clear with how it hung on one of her shoulders that there was padding and bandages underneath.

He slid into the chair opposite them and Sophie smiled, before going away to give them some privacy.

"I'm sorry mom. I never meant to hurt you." He said quietly, his voice barely a whisper.

"It's alright, these things happen..." She said, as if she herself wasn't certain.

Surprisingly, his dad laughed.

"These things happen? You mean you've got shot before? Care to tell us the story dear?" His dad said.

Marcus couldn't help it, a grin snuck across his face.

His mother rolled her eyes and adjusted the blazer slightly.

"Funny. Now, how are you finding it hear Marcus? They've told us about your diagnosis... We should have known something was up... I'm so sorry darling." She said, sighing.

His mother sounded distraught and Marcus finally felt like he had his mother and father again. They weren't imposters; they were parents that overlooked something and were doing their best.

"It's not bad actually. I... I'm sorry I shot you... I wanted to... to end my life... Not hurt you." He said.

It felt strange forming the words; a part of him struggled to even remember it properly; all of it had gone a little hazy as if his brain was refusing with him to say that it was real.

Yet it was real, it had really happened and he had hurt the people he cared about most. His mother stared at him empathetically and she reached out and grabbed his wrist, holding it tightly.

"I'm glad we were able to get you help, before you did. You are the most important thing in the world to us both, if you were gone, I don't know what I'd do with myself." She said.

Marcus smiled at her and felt his eyes watering with tears.

"I love you both. I'm sorry." He said.

"We love you too son, now what's important is you listen to everything the Doctor says so that we can get you out of here and playing soccer again okay? Everything will be fine." His father said, smiling.

Marcus nodded and smiled back. If his parents didn't hate him for what he was, then there was no way that he could possibly hate himself for this either.

*

"Thirty days..." Marcus murmured uncertainly to himself.

He had been in the facility for thirty days exactly and today was the day that he was getting dismissed and sent home. The mental health hospital had been the help and support he needed, but he feared going back to school and what everyone would say.

Sophie, the kind nurse, had been especially supportive and proud of him for doing everything they'd asked during his time there. He'd taken the medicine, he'd explained his symptoms well and he'd even seen his parents and met with them, the nurse and the doctor to find a therapist in the city he could start seeing as well as taking the medication.

Marcus was terrified, but he knew that he was ready to start living again. The last month or so had been a blur – it had felt like he had lost who he truly was and trying to find his way back had been like walking through quicksand – like any moment he was about to be pulled back into the delusions he knew weren't real but found so difficult to fight.

His parents arrived outside of the hospital and the nurse hugged him as he got into the car. It was strange, watching the city of Columbus rush by as he went back home – somewhere that he hadn't seen in so long. His parents had kindly brought him a change of clothes as well, which he had changed into back in the facility before leaving. He was wearing one of his football shirts with some jeans, but it felt strange putting something other than hospital clothes on.

Slowly, his mother pulled into the driveway of the large house and came to a stop.

"You ready champ?" His dad said turning around.

Marcus swallowed and nodded uncertainly. His parents opened the side door and they all strode to the house.

They pushed Marcus through first and Marcus was aghast when he opened the door.

"SURPRISE!"

All of his friends were in the hallway and one of them was holding a large "get better soon!" sign. Taken aback, Marcus seemed to almost leap in shock.

Slowly, as he realized that his friends were in fact there to support him, and his struggle – and his parents had planned this party to welcome him back home.

He smiled and then went straight to the lounge to find a large, food platter as everyone went about enjoying the small party.

Looking around, he noticed that one person, which he definitely owed an apology was stood, inspecting some mini-sandwiches carefully.

"Hey..." Marcus said quietly.

Jerimiah looked at him for a moment and then smiled, patting him on the back.

"Hey, your parents threw a great party. You should shoot your mom more often." He said.

Marcus snorted and looked at his feet.

"I'm sorry that I acted so weird... I was going through a lot..." He said, looking down at his feet.

"It's fine man. I know we don't talk about stuff much, but we can totally do so. It must've been hard getting help about things and I don't know what I'd have done if I lost you.

I'm sorry I didn't come to visit... I was kind of scared to see you in that place and I wasn't sure you wanted to see me. You're my best friend though and I'm glad you're al good now." He said.

Marcus smiled at him and then pulled him into a hug.

"Thanks for being my friend." Marcus said quietly. Jerimiah slapped him on the back and squeezed him back.

"You seen Marianne? I need to talk to her..." Marcus said, looking around.

Jerimiah pointed him in the direction of the kitchen and Marcus took a deep breath, before going to find her.

Marianne looked breath-taking as usual. She was wearing a gorgeous pink-sparkled dress that glimmered as she walked and a pair of slip-ons. She looked around the kitchen, biting her lip as she was looking for something.

"Hey..." Marcus said.

She turned around, blushing.

"Hey Marcus..."

"What are you looking for? Maybe I can help?"

"Just a glass to get some water, there's only fizzy drinks in the longue and at that little table, but I just want some water."

Marcus nodded and went to the cabinet where the glasses were stored and then poured her a glass of water. He watched her carefully as she sipped away.

"Did I miss the formal?" He asked casually, trying to mask the fear that was bubbling inside of him.

"No, actually they ended up postponing it because of a couple of things that happened... But I'm not going to go into that. It's next week actually." She said, sipping the water timidly as her bright eyes watched him.

"Well... Uh... If it's been postponed and it's next week. Do you want to go together?" He asked nervously, shifting from foot to foot as he awaited her answer.

"Yes. I would love too." She said grinning at him. She then bounded up to him and hugged him tightly, planting a kiss on his cheek.

"I'm really glad you're back and you're okay. I missed you Marcus. It was really scary seeing you act like that and not knowing if you were okay. You're really brave. I like you and I can't wait to go to the formal with you." She gently drew away from him and smiled, going out of the kitchen to join the rest of the party.

Marcus gently touched his cheek where she had kissed it and blushed with a smile. Glad to have finally got the one thing he'd been wanting for so many years – a date with Marianne and the chance to ask her to be his girlfriend.

~ 9 ~

A MEANS TO AN END

"That was the crux. You. Only you could work on you. Nobody could force you, and if you weren't ready, then you weren't ready, and no amount of open-armed encouragement was going to change that." — *Norah Vincent*

Marcus' life became pretty boring when he went back to school. He became more involved in math with Miss Callie's help and ended up joining the math team, with the coach's gentle encouragement he'd also started training more and had achieved his star status again.

Yet, the thing he was most proud of was that he had decided to found a peer support group in the school with help from his parents. It was a mental health group for anyone with mental health problems and they would sit in a circle, talk about their own experiences and coping mechanisms every Thursday lunch time.

There were a few seniors and juniors that had tentatively applied that he didn't recognize and that had started attending. In a way he was thankful that he didn't recognize them, it was easier to talk about where he had gotten where he was with strangers.

Then, some of his friends joined and he was surprised to learn of their difficulties. Tyler had always been a friend that was quiet;

he never let the other kids go to his house and he never spoke about his home life.

Surprisingly, during lunchtime, when Marcus asked if anyone would like to speak or share anything about their experiences, Tyler raised his hand.

"I lost my mom a couple of years ago. My dad yells at me every night and tells me it's my fault. It's hard. I miss her." He said sadly, and slunk down in his seat.

Marcus was taken aback, he would never had guessed such a thing from knowing Tyler as long as he had; after all being reserved for as long as he had been around him and his other friends – Marcus had actually assumed it was more of a feminine quality and that he was quite close to his mother.

Yet, that was further from the truth, he watched on in shock and then managed to compose himself as he cleared his throat.

"Thank you for sharing, um... Has anyone had any similar experiences? Maybe you can share some advice for Tyler here..."

Sure enough, to Marcus' surprise there were two other students who had also lost parents and spoke about how they coped with it in their own ways.

Marcus presumed that it would only be just the one friend he would see at the support group, but the following week, he found Maury. Then Alexi. Then most shockingly of all, about a month later George joined.

*

After a full three months of when the formal was going to take place, it had finally been given a proper date and it fell tonight. Marianne had still promised to go with Marcus, even though it had been cancelled many a time.

In fact, she had been eager to go with him, after each cancellation and each new date, she had checked in with him to ask if he still wanted to go. Which led to tonight.

His mother watched as Marcus descended the stairs nervously and she started taking non-stop pictures of him. Grinning to herself and gushing over how handsome he looked.

Marcus turned away embarrassed and then saw something hanging in the hallway.

"Um, what is that doing there?" He asked, trying to stop the mortification from overwhelming him.

His mother smiled at him and looked at the painting.

Marcus had – at the recommendation of his therapist which he saw twice a week – had asked him to start drawing and painting. He found some videos of a really calming man that walked through how to do peaceful scenes in a very polite and soft tone.

It had been a great way to keep Marcus relaxed on particularly stressful days (like the finals which were coming up next week...) and he had been doing the tutorials since.

His mother had clearly found one of the paintings and it sat on the hallway proudly in a frame.

"Think about how far you've come in the last six months. I'm proud of you and your father is as well. That shows not only how far you've come but how well you're able to work on coping mechanisms and ways to handle stress. I'm so proud of you darling." She said and threw her arms around him.

"Mom! Stop! You're going to mess up my hair..." He said, peeling himself off her. She chuckled to herself and let go, snapping a few more pictures before they both exited to drive to the formal at school.

*

As soon as Marcus entered, he saw Marianne waiting. She was wearing a gorgeous red dress that seemed to shimmer in the lights that the school had up. A smile danced on her face; and she looked radiant.

Nervousness was booming inside of Marcus, he felt like he had eaten some live snakes and they were currently writhing in his stomach. He bit his lip, but quickly stopped and breathed in and out of ten seconds, just like his therapist taught him too and then walked over to her.

"You look gorgeous..." He said, gently putting his hand on her waist.

She turned and looked up at him, her eyes sparkling in the lights and she pulled him onto the dancefloor.

"Listen... Marianne, there's something I've been wanting to ask you for a very long time." He said, wondering if his fear was about to clamp over his words and drown them.

"Yes? You dance really well by the way!" She said, as they swayed on the dancefloor.

"Thanks... I um... I... I really like you. I've known you for a very long time, but I've liked you for as long as I can remember. I've been thinking of this moment for awhile, and how I'd say it, what I'd do... I'm not good at big romantic things... But...

Will you be my girlfriend?" He asked nervously.

The whole world seemed to stop for a moment, as he waited for an answer. She looked up at him, the lights of the school hall dancing across her face as they swayed together.

It was strange how a single moment could last an entire eternity, yet for a moment Marcus felt like he was trapped, doomed to never know her answer.

To his surprise, her face lit up and she said the one thing that he had been dying to hear.

"Yes!"

With that, they swayed together for the rest of the dance and Marcus smiled, knowing he had a girl who accepted him for what he suffered with, he had friends that loved him no matter what and he was getting help.

Resources

Mental health is every where in today's society and we live in a world that stigmatizes mental health and works hard to make people feel like they're crazy. This book aims to break down those barriers that society has built up. You are not crazy. You are valued. You are worthy of help.

Below is some places that you can find help/resources if you or a loved one is struggling with any of the issues that have been mentioned in this book.

Schizophrenia

- https://www.rethink.org/advice-and-information/about-mental-illness/learn-more-about-conditions/schizophrenia/?gclid=Cj0KCQiA0fr_BRDaARIsAABw4EtyhOWV5Sg-AJIZn4myQ6IuyKKd4U7-bxdhGxZUc9LE_FcuwS-O2jcaAsDvEALw_wcB
- https://www.psychiatry.org/patients-families/schizophrenia

Anxiety

- https://www.mind.org.uk/information-support/types-of-mental-health-problems/anxiety-and-panic-attacks/anxiety-treatments/

- https://www.cci.health.wa.gov.au/Resources/Looking-After-Yourself/Anxiety

Depression

- https://www.healthline.com/health/depression/help-for-depression

Eating disorders

- https://www.beateatingdisorders.org.uk/support-services/downloads-resources

- http://www.eatingdisorderssupport.co.uk/help/links-resources

Suicidal thoughts

- Call 1-800-273-8255 immediately

- https://www.healthline.com/health/mental-health/sui-cide-resource-guide
- https://www.nimh.nih.gov/health/topics/suicide-preven-tion/index.shtml

Recovery Position:

- https://www.nhs.uk/conditions/first-aid/recovery-posi-tion/

Above all else. Remember that you are not alone in your struggles. We all have something that we are working on and it can seem impossible. Be there for one another and do not afraid to be human. Together we can fight the stigma against mental health, and grow together- Brennan Lehotay MSN, RN, PMH-BC

CPSIA information can be obtained
at www.ICGtesting.com
Printed in the USA
LVHW050940200221
679499LV00035B/582